His eyes g̶ strangely at her...

But Rafael spoke smoothly, "You won't be allowed to go anywhere without *my* permission!"

Victoria's gasp of outrage was met with his cool statement, "You are now once again my wife, and here a husband's commands to his wife are the next best thing to law."

Collecting herself, and with equally cool defiance, she told her husband, through lips stiff with anger, "I won't put up with this! I'm not a chattel, and I'll go to England if I want to!"

The gleam in Rafael's eyes intensified. "Try *señora*. Without a passport, you will get nowhere. No, you will stay here and be a proper wife to me—as I recall you once enjoyed very much, indeed...."

WELCOME
TO THE WONDERFUL WORLD
OF *Harlequin Romances*

Interesting, informative and entertaining,
each Harlequin Romance portrays an appealing
and original love story. With a varied array
of settings, we may lure you on an African safari,
to a quaint Welsh village, or an exotic Riviera
location—anywhere and everywhere that adventurous
men and women fall in love.

As publishers of Harlequin Romances, we're
extremely proud of our books. Since 1949,
Harlequin Enterprises has built its publishing
reputation on the solid base of quality and
originality. Our stories are the most popular
paperback romances sold in North America; every
month, six new titles are released and sold at
nearly every book-selling store in Canada and the
United States.

A free catalogue listing all Harlequin Romances
can be yours by writing to the

HARLEQUIN READER SERVICE,
(In the U.S.) 1440 South Priest Drive, Tempe, AZ 85281
(In Canada) Stratford, Ontario, N5A 6W2

We sincerely hope you enjoy reading
this Harlequin Romance.

Yours truly,

THE PUBLISHERS
  Harlequin Romances

The Bright Side of Dark

by

JENETH MURREY

Harlequin Books

TORONTO • LONDON • LOS ANGELES • AMSTERDAM
SYDNEY • HAMBURG • PARIS • STOCKHOLM • ATHENS • TOKYO

Original hardcover edition published in 1981
by Mills & Boon Limited

ISBN 0-373-02470-3

Harlequin edition published April 1982

CHAPTER ONE

THE stars gleamed down on her, pale and cold, pricking through the blackness overhead, and she was relieved to find that they no longer spun in crazy cartwheels each time she looked at them. The vicious, clamouring pain which racked her body was fading and a cold numbness was creeping up from her feet. Soon it would reach her head, she thought, and then nothing would hurt her any more. Her hand scrabbled weakly in loose stone chippings, there was grass beneath her cheek and the smell of damp earth in her nostrils. She tried to move her head to a more comfortable position, but the effort brought a cruel stabbing pain that caused the cold stars to wheel again in the black velvet of the sky, and she lost consciousness.

She knew nothing of the headlights which later shone on her where she lay, half in, half out of the shallow ditch; nor of the careful hands that lifted her on to the stretcher. She recovered consciousness sufficiently to be vaguely grateful for the rough woollen blanket that covered her. The numbness had brought with it a creeping cold that seeped through her body, making her shiver uncontrollably. There was a sharp sting in her arm and she slid away into a deep, silent pool of blackness.

Later, the pool became full of nightmarish happenings. There were bright lights that shone on her and seagulls that swooped and swayed above her, pecking viciously at her head. A dark face with big crystal eyes came close to her, little painful lights shone into her eyes and an invisible person picked up her hand and deliberately broke it before tying it to the ground.

She struggled up out of the stifling darkness into a warm, deep peace. The loose chippings, the grass and the damp earth were gone. There was a soft smoothness under her body and head, a smoothness that smelled of soap and disinfectant with overtones of ether. A hospital smell. Why then was there a seagull hovering beside her? Soon another seagull came and for long minutes the two birds fluttered, one on each side of her. With relief, she saw them fly away.

Beneath the small light at the end of the ward, Sister Maria Immaculata paused to make an entry in her night book. She turned to bid Sister Catalina goodnight, saying that their new patient's pulse was much stronger now and nodding with satisfaction. The nod of her head caused the wide white wings of her coif to sway and flutter like the wings of some great bird.

The morning sun poked curious fingers through the gap in the screens around the bed, lighting up the pillow and sliding across the girl's closed eyelids. The brightness woke her from a deep peace into a throbbing, painful world. Experimentally, she tried moving her limbs, but when further pain shot through her, she lay still, hardly daring to breathe. Her head ached abominably and her mouth felt dry and gritty. A seagull swooped above her and with an effort she concentrated upon it. It wasn't a seagull at all. It was the wide white coif of a nun of the Sister of Mercy order and from under the starched linen a round, rosy face smiled at her.

'Thirsty,' she croaked. The cold rim of a cup was pressed against her mouth and a cool liquid flowed in. It trickled down her throat, soothing and refreshing. She smiled back at the plump, smiling face, trying to say 'Thank you', but no words came.

Time passed in this way for two days. She slept and woke, drank and slept again until the third morning when she woke to find the pain nearly gone and her thoughts no longer fuzzy. There was a dull ache in her head and she found that it took a great deal of effort to move, even to raise her head or her hand. Otherwise she felt quite well, even cheerful. The screens had been moved from around her bed and folded back so that she could see all the ward.

She gazed around appreciatively. The first thing that struck her was the almost Spartan cleanliness. The floorboards were polished and shone with a dark golden glow, the walls were washed white and were quite unadorned except for a large, dark wooden crucifix over the door. There were only six beds in the ward, each rigidly immaculate under a spotless white counterpane, and of these only two were occupied—hers and the bed nearest the door which contained a heavy-looking middle-aged woman with sharp black eyes, several double chins and the suspicion of a moustache on her upper lip.

Her small amount of movement must have been noticed, for almost at once a white-coiffed nun in a blue-grey habit came to the side of the bed, pleasure and something suspiciously like relief shining out of her large dark eyes. This was not the little rosy-faced one who had given her drinks. This nun was tall and almost painfully thin, but her ivory-coloured face was calm and her magnificent black eyes were serene under an unlined brow.

'Ah! You wake, *señora*.' The nun's English was good but heavily accented. 'You would like a drink?' Cool, fresh lemon juice flowed down her throat like nectar and then she was lifted in the bed, her hands and face washed and her long copper-coloured hair was gently brushed and replaited.

She winced with pain in her head, 'Sister,' she asked, 'where am I—what happened?'

Sister Maria Immaculata gently pushed her back against the pillows. 'You are at the House of Mercy, which is a small hospital run by our order. It is about five miles outside Pamplona and you have been here for three days,' she explained gently. 'There was an automobile crash and you were found and brought here with concussion, a head wound and a broken arm and wrist, but everything is now healing well. In a few days the stitches will be removed from your head and in about a month the plaster will be removed from your arm and be replaced with a softer, less weighty support.'

Her patient looked with interest at the plaster that weighed down her left arm. It extended to more than half way up to her elbow and right down to her knuckles, and it felt like a ton weight on her arm.

'Now,' Sister Maria Immaculata surveyed her patient with a degree of satisfaction as she straightened a minute crease in the counterpane, 'do you think you could answer a few questions?'

'Yes, of course,' replied her patient. 'What is it you want to know?'

'Firstly, your name, for our records, you understand, and also because we do not know what to call you, which we find uncomfortable. Also, we must notify your family.'

'My name is Victoria. I don't have it shortened,' she explained, 'so you must call me Victoria.'

'And your other names?' Sister Maria Immaculata had produced a ballpoint pen and was holding it poised to fill in the empty spaces on the temperature and blood pressure chart.

Victoria hesitated, a frown wrinkling her surprisingly dark eyebrows. There was an uncomfortable pause, then, 'I'm sorry, but I can't tell you that. Oh no,' as she caught sight of the bewildered look in the tall nun's eyes, 'I'm not trying to hide anything. I just don't know. The "Victoria" was easy, but when I try to go on, there's nothing there. I can't remember anything more, just Victoria.' She tried to keep her voice steady, but without much success. Fear was cramping her stomach.

Sister Maria Immaculata wrote 'Victoria' in the empty space. Her ears had registered the hoarseness of her patient's still weak voice. Her eyes had noticed the nervous clenching of Victoria's hand on the counterpane, had also seen the faint film of perspiration on the pale face. She smiled gently and said in a calm, soothing voice, 'It will be the concussion, I expect. Often this happens with head injuries, the patient is confused and has difficulty remembering a few things. Can you tell me where you live?'

Victoria thought hard, but there was a stupid blank in her mind—a frightening blank. Not trusting herself to speak in case rising hysteria showed in her voice, she shook her head.

'There is no need to worry,' Sister Maria Immaculata's voice flowed over her like a soothing lotion. 'We thought something like this might happen. Relax now and rest. I will bring you some soup—you must be very hungry by this time and to be hungry is no help, is it?' She restored the pen to a clip on the chart board, smiled down at the pale face against the pillows and serenely went off to find the soup.

Victoria obediently lay back against the pillows but relaxation was impossible as also was rest. She searched around in her memory, but it was a complete blank, like a room which had been stripped of furniture to stand empty and echoing. She could remember the starlight and the pain, but that was as far back as she could go. She became very cross with herself. This was stupid, utterly stupid! She hadn't started living just a few days ago in this hospital. There must be years and years for her to remember. Where had those years gone? Constructive thought! That was what was needed in a situation like this. What did she know?

She reviewed her mind. She was in a hospital outside Pamplona, Pamplona was in Spain, therefore she was in

Spain. Now that was sensible; she felt quite pleased with herself. Now to progress in a similar logical fashion on the name problem. My name is Victoria, I can't remember any other name, but I must have one, everybody has two names. I would have the same name as my parents, and my father's name was. ... She ran up against the blank wall of nothingness again. Tears of vexation and fright rose in her eyes and spilled over so that when the chubby little white-coated doctor came to the bedside, he found a weeping young woman who was trembling with fright.

'Ah no!' He was very firm. 'The *señora* must not distress herself in this way, it can only do harm. The memory is a fickle thing. When one reaches for it, it runs away. If one ignores it, it will soon reappear.'

The *señora* glared at him through her tears. Ridiculous man! How could she help but distress herself? Here she was in a foreign country, knowing nothing and nobody, not even how she had come here and when. Perhaps she was a tourist? 'My passport,' she asked. 'Where is my passport?'

The doctor gave a little, very Latin shrug and spread his pudgy fingers. 'The car in which you were travelling, *señora*, it crashed, the petrol tank exploded and all was totally consumed in the fire. All your possessions were consumed with it, your clothing, your papers. , . .' Again came the shrug and the spread fingers.

'My companions?' Victoria asked breathlessly. 'What happened to them, were they killed?'

The doctor shook his head regretfully. 'You were travelling alone, *señora*. There were no companions, but you must not worry unduly. The car will eventually be identified and then all will be well. The car could then be traced through the police channels, so you must rest and regain your strength. See, here comes Sister Maria Immaculata with some nourishing soup.' He patted Victoria's hand and left as the Sister arrived.

The soup was hot and fragrant, giving off a delicious aroma of chicken and herbs. Victoria swallowed every drop. Weariness descended upon her when she had finished the last of it so that as the nun wiped her patient's mouth with a snowy napkin, Victoria's eyes were closing. Within a few minutes she was fast asleep and did not therefore hear the serious note in the doctor's voice as he came back to speak to the nun.

'Amnesia. It could be temporary or permanent. We have no means of knowing and there is no treatment that we can give. In large modern hospitals sometimes they have success with hypnosis, but here. . . .' He shrugged. 'We can only heal the body. The mind . . . that we must leave to God. No excitement, Sister. Rest and quiet.'

'We will pray for her.' Sister Maria Immaculata smiled serenely and the doctor trotted off.

Two days passed in tranquillity. Victoria's mind was quite easy. Once the car had been identified and traced, she would have a name, an identity. Meanwhile, she would wait, and the waiting was easy. She grew to love the little hospital ward, the quiet peace. Sister Maria Immaculata's gentle calm and the rosy cheeks and merry eyes of Sister Catalina who shared the duties with her.

The two nuns were such opposite characters. Little Sister Catalina chattered of other patients, the beauties of Navarre and her family; unlike Sister Maria Immaculata who was of a noble family in Andalusia and was more reserved, Sister Catalina hailed from the small town of Lecumberi; she was one of a large family of sturdy peasant stock. She displayed her hands, large and strong, reddened and roughened with continual scrubbing and cleaning.

'The hands of Sister Maria Immaculata,' she whispered, 'are of a slimness and whiteness that no amount of strong soap can spoil. They are good hands for soothing a fretful patient, for cleaning a wound or for comforting a fretful child. Me, I like to talk to people, to hear their troubles and to make the little jokes so that people will laugh and feel well again.'

On the sixteenth day of Victoria's stay in the hospital, Sister Catalina came running, an air of suppressed excitement surrounding her like an outsize halo. She carried with her a large woollen shawl, the product of somebody's clever fingers with a crochet hook.

'Is it not beautiful, *señora*? See the workmanship, so fine, and the pattern of leaves, so expertly executed. Now I must wash you and tidy your hair. You must be made beautiful also, for you have a visitor.'

Victoria sat bolt upright in bed. 'They've traced the car?' she asked. 'They've discovered who I am?' At Sister Catalina's emphatic nod, tears of relief filled her eyes. At last she was a real person again! Somebody knew her, she was not alone in the world. Her fears, choked down and suppressed for thirteen days, spilled over into a flood of happy tears which flowed freely, pouring down her cheeks.

Sister Catalina tut-tutted. 'No more,' she begged. 'No more tears. We have prayed for you, and see, our prayers have been answered.' While she chatted, her hands were busy. Victoria's hands and face were sponged and patted dry, her hair was brushed and braided into two plaits which were tied at the bottom with small pieces of narrow bandage. Her nightgown was changed for a clean one and the shawl was arranged about her shoulders. Pillows were stuffed behind her back so that she was supported in a sitting position, and finally Sister Catalina pronounced herself satisfied.

The screens about the bed prevented Victoria from seeing the little procession which came up the ward. She had to wait until Sister Catalina parted them to let in first the doctor and then another man. Involuntarily, Victoria gasped and grasped the little nun's hand, her fingers pressing into the flesh. Her heart was beating hard, so hard that the blood drummed in her ears and she found breathing difficult.

The little doctor beamed at her, taking her plastered arm and patting the tips of her fingers exposed below the plaster and then pressing them firmly with his own.

'All is well, *señora*, as I told you it would be. The car was identified, the Guardia have been very swift about it and it was at once traced to its owner. So now we know who you are! This, *señora*,' he gestured to the tall, silent figure, 'this is your husband!'

Shock made her sway back against the pillows. Her husband! She found difficulty in withdrawing her gaze from the doctor's face, covered as it was by a fatuous grin. A stupid, fatuous grin, as if he had done something very clever and was inordinately pleased with himself! What had he got to be pleased about? Presenting her with a husband as he would have presented her with a box of chocolates. She didn't know anything about a husband. A father or mother perhaps, that she could have accepted, or a brother or sister, even a friend, but a husband! She raised stormy eyes and looked at this husband.

'I do not know you, *señor*,' she said in a high clear voice. 'There's some mistake. I've never seen you before.'

The doctor looked startled, then a serious look spread over his plump, dark features. He began to speak, explaining.

Victoria paid no attention to him, her gaze remained on the man standing lazily against the foot of the bed. Very tall and slim, he oozed arrogance and something else which she could not place at the moment. He had black hair, brushed firmly back from his forehead, hair that was slightly silvered at the temples. It would curl or wave, she thought if he wasn't so ruthless with it. His face was a dark olive hue and the dark eyes, under his strongly marked brows glittered nastily.

Her gaze travelled on down, past an imperious beak of a nose, over a thin-lipped, cruel-looking mouth, the lower lip of which was sensuously curved, over a masterful chin. Her eyes continued to descend, past the superbly cut and tailored suiting that covered his broad-shouldered frame, the cream silk shirt with a symphonic tie. The end of her bed cut off the rest of her view, otherwise she could have gone on down to his shoes, hand-stitched, she guessed, and impeccably polished. He breathed money.

Her eyes returned to his face. His eyes still glittered and she noticed that his nostrils were pinched in as if he was restraining himself. That was it! Arrogance, she thought and anger. A well controlled but nevertheless, icy rage. He had been brought here and confronted with her as his wife. No wonder he was angry!

'I'm sorry that you've had a wasted journey, *señor*.' She managed to keep the wobble out of her voice. 'I hope you've not had to travel far.'

The little doctor was babbling away about identification and Victoria ignored him for as long as she could, but finally she was forced to turn to him. Sadly, almost, she shook her head. 'I'm sorry, doctor,' she muttered. He patted her hand again, growing excited.

'But, *señora*, there *is* no mistake. The description— you were described!'

'Pooh!' Victoria snorted, her courage returning. 'Descriptions are never accurate. . . .' A lazy voice interrupted her in mid-flight.

'And how many redheaded English girls do you think would be driving *my* car, *querida*? Driving *my* car in the direction of *my* home?'

Victoria's mouth became a round 'O' and her eyes widened with shock as she met his gaze. A slight, a very slight movement of the black head sent the little doctor scurrying outside the screens.

'And now, Victoria, shall we cease playing games?'

His eyes were glittering dangerously. 'You have some explaining to do and I advise you that you begin now. You will tell me why you went without my permission. That will do to begin with.'

Her own anger rose, suppressing the cold little fear that crawled in her stomach.

'I've told you, *señor*, I don't know you. To the best of my knowledge, I've never seen you before in my life.' She turned to Sister Catalina, surprising a sympathetic expression on the rosy face. 'Sister, please send him away, there's been some terrible mistake. . . .' Her anger was evaporating fast, taking with it all her courage, and she felt beaten and cowed. All she wanted was that they should all go away and leave her alone so that she could have a good cry.

A wave of sorrow swept over her and disappointment brought tears to her eyes. Swiftly he was at the side of the bed, his arm warm about her shoulders, pulling her gently but firmly against him. Victoria found the arm very comforting, so comforting that she buried her face in his expensive jacket and sobbed noisily for several minutes. When the spasm had passed and she grew calmer, she raised a tear-streaked face to him.

'I'm sorry, *señor*,' she gulped, 'but I had such hopes. It's been dreadful, lying here, not knowing who I am. I thought I would see somebody that I knew, that I recognised, and everything would come flooding back. I thought you would be somebody I knew.' She managed a brief watery smile. 'You've been kind and I'm sorry that I'm such a nuisance to everyone.' Several hiccups interrupted her attempt at an apology.

He lifted a stray lock of hair which had fallen across her face and smoothed it back gently. He also produced an immaculate handkerchief and mopped up her wet face before he removed his supporting arm and pressed her back on to the pillows. She looked up at him from under eyelids, puffy with weeping. He wasn't angry any more. The dark eyes no longer glittered savagely and his hard mouth had softened slightly. There was even the suspicion of a smile, she thought, a very small smile tucked into the firm corners of his mouth and in the deep creases of his cheeks. Victoria gave a little sigh of relief. She had needed that outburst, needed a shoulder to cry on.

'Rest for a little while, *querida*. I must speak with the doctors. When I have done that, I will return, if it is permitted. When you feel more calm and able, we will have a little talk.'

His place was taken by Sister Catalina, who chirruped with distress at Victoria's tear-blurred features. She fetched water and in a few minutes had restored both Victoria and the bed to a state of pristine freshness. Victoria lay, clutching the large male handkerchief which smelled faintly of a very expensive cologne, trying to make some sense out of the senseless things that were happening to her. It was all a ghastly muddle, there was no rhyme or reason to it.

The effort of trying to sort out her chaotic thoughts made her head ache and she lifted her hand and ran her finger along the line of the scar on her head. Under the dressing and bandage she could feel the lumps where the stitches had been. There seemed to be a great many of them and the wound ran in a curve from her temple down to behind her left ear. She gave a little groan and closed her eyes; she would try to sleep. Perhaps when she woke, this waking nightmare she was living in would have gone away and everything would be sweetly sane and reasonable again.

Victoria opened her eyes to find Sister Maria Immaculata by the bedside with a bowl of soup and a fresh, crusty roll of bread. It must be past six o'clock in the evening, then, because that was when Sister Catalina went off duty. He, the man who said he was her husband, would have gone by now. He hadn't come back

to see her, and she felt a sweet relief. She wanted time—
time to think of what to do, but what could she do
except lie here and lap up soup or tortillas or salad or
whatever they cared to stuff down her.

She ate the soup slowly but refused anything else, and
after obediently swallowing two white tablets, she found
herself drifting off into a lovely haze full of soft woolly
clouds, where things like amnesia, husbands and being
lost didn't matter a bit.

The next morning she woke feeling very sorry for
herself. It was the effect of the pills, she was told. They
were a mild tranquilliser and often left the patient in a
depressed state, but after she had been washed and had
partaken of hot coffee with perhaps a roll and jam, she
would feel better. Victoria glowered at little Sister
Catalina, but one look at the plump face, the dark eyes
so full of sympathy and understanding, made her feel
very mean and small. Hesitantly, she tried to apologise,
but her apology was dismissed with the wave of a work-
worn hand.

'But we expect this!' Sister Catalina smiled with enthusiasm. 'You are getting better, regaining your
strength. When this happens, the patient is often irrit-
able and peevish. It is a good sign.' Carefully she inspected Victoria's head wound and pronounced herself
satisfied. 'There is no more need of the dressing or bandage. Everything is healed.' Sister Catalina was solicitous. 'Very little of your hair has been cut, and you have
so much! And already it is growing again. A few weeks
and it will be as if it never happened. There will be no
marks at all.'

Under Sister Catalina's ministrations, Victoria began
to feel better. The hot, fragrant coffee revived her and
she bit into a warm roll with enjoyment while the nun
bustled about, taking her pulse, temperature and blood
pressure and then making sure that there was nothing
out of place. As if anything could be out of place,

Victoria thought, when it was all tidied, dusted and arranged about fifteen times a day!

In the afternoon, the screens were once more placed around her bed. Through a small gap in them she saw a short, swarthy man come in and go to the other woman in the ward. The door closed behind him and didn't open again. Visiting time, obviously, and just as obviously there were no visitors for her. *He* had not come back, and yet she had been almost sure that he would. Disappointment was almost a physical pain in her chest. Here she was, washed and brushed, the shawl draped across her shoulders, and nobody to come and see her. She felt like an abandoned dog. Anyone would have done, even *him*.

Her miserable thoughts were disturbed by the sound of the door being opened and a murmur of conversation. She peeped through the gap and was rewarded by the sight of not just one visitor but five. They weren't all truly visitors, though. In the lead was the tall, dark stranger who claimed to be her husband, accompanied by a very senior doctor, then came another doctor and the matron, a little birdlike woman who was not a nun. Victoria had seen her before on her tours of inspection and had admired the shining, scrubbed efficiency of her. From the topmost frill of her starched lawn cap to the twinkling toes of her polished shoes, she was perfection. Not a hair was ever out of place and her sharp black eyes darted, positively looking for a creased sheet or a wrinkled bedcover.

Sister Catalina brought up the rear of the procession, but must have done some pretty nifty footwork while they were hidden from Victoria's sight, because it was she who parted the screens to admit this exalted company. A further hurried step brought the fat little doctor, Dr Sanchez, into the gathering, with a large file in his hand. The three doctors then had a consultation, passing the file from hand to hand like a parcel in a Christmas game.

Meanwhile, the man who claimed to be her husband came and sat beside her and took her hand in his, thus giving, she thought, a lovely picture of husbandly devotion. He smiled at her gently and stroked her thumb, saying nothing until his escort, apparently satisfied with her progress, departed, all of them except for Dr Sanchez, who took a seat on the other side of the bed and Sister Catalina who hovered out of earshot on the other side of the screens.

'I still don't believe it!' Victoria told them. 'I *can't* believe it! I've thought about it all morning and it doesn't make sense.' Her husband raised an eyebrow in mute query. 'If you are my husband,' she explained carefully, 'why did it take so long for you to come here and find me?' Little Dr Sanchez prepared to break into speech, but an authoritative gesture from the other side of the bed stopped him.

'*Querida*, listen for a few moments.' He sounded exasperated. 'Three weeks ago we were all to go to Lourdes. No!' he laid a long finger on her lips. 'The why of it is unimportant for the moment. Unfortunately, I was called to Santander, a matter of business which could not wait. You, Victoria, I suppose not wishing to disappoint Isabel, decided that you would drive them there yourself. So you, together with Isabel, Abuela and Inez, drove to Lourdes by way of St Jean de Luz and Pau. You were all supposed to stay for a week, but after four days, when I returned hom from Santander, Abuela telephoned. She was much surprised to hear that you were not at home. She told me that you had spent but one night at Lourdes and had left before noon the day after your arrival there, to come home, she understood. What she did not tell me, because she did not know herself, was that when you drove back, you crossed the border at St Jean Pied de Port. You had taken another route, and it was not far from there, in the Pass at

Roncevalles, that the car crashed. Mercifully, you were either thrown out or you crawled to safety before the petrol tank exploded, setting all on fire.'

'I don't know, I can't remember.' Nervously Victoria licked lips suddenly dry with fear. 'But if you knew, why didn't you come before? That's what I can't understand.'

'It is all true, *señora*,' Dr Sanchez assured her. 'As the Señor has said, you returned to Spain by a route which he had not envisaged. The car was totally consumed by flames and it took some days for it to be identified and your husband to be notified. Also remember, *señora*, that until the telephone call four days after the accident, the Señor assumed that you were safe at Lourdes with the rest of your party. The only person who could have helped the police and the Guardia was yourself, and you could not do that.'

Victoria closed her eyes. It was all so sensible, so reasonable. Why couldn't she believe it? Because you don't want to, said a little voice inside her head. When she opened her eyes again, the doctor had gone, leaving her alone with her husband. He seemed to be amused about something, and she became cross.

'You seem to find this amusing, *señor*. I wish you would share the joke, because I can't find anything even remotely funny about it.'

'It is yourself, little one. You behave like a small wild animal caught in a trap. You shiver and moan, yet when somebody tries to release you, you growl and snap at the fingers which mean only to help you. Can you not understand? We mean only to help.' He stood up and stooped over the bed, taking her face between his hands and forcing her to look at him. 'Trust me, *querida*. You have nothing to fear.' She felt his lips touch her forehead and then he was gone—and she didn't even know his name!

Sister Catalina came and chattered. 'I am so happy

for you, *señora*, so very happy! Now you will see that all will be well. It is good, is it not, to cast one's burdens upon stronger shoulders than one's own, and your husband, *señora*, his shoulders look very strong. Now all that remains is for you to get well.'

Sister Maria Immaculata brought her evening meal, succulent slices of chicken with fluffy rice followed by fruit. Also there was a small case, the Señor had brought it for her comfort. When Victoria had disposed of her chicken and rice and had wiped the last traces of peach juice from her lips and chin, she and the Sister inspected the contents of the case. Two pairs of thick silk pyjamas and a green velvet robe pleased her enormously; the white cotton smocks which the hospital provided were much too big. There was a pair of soft green slippers, soap, hankies, toothbrush and toothpaste, a brush and comb, a box of tissues, a jar of face cream, even a bottle of cologne. Best of all, there were two magazines and a Georgette Heyer novel.

Victoria crowed with delight and insisted on donning a pair of the pyjamas at once, together with the slippers and the robe, and then wheedled Sister Maria Immaculata into helping her out of bed for her daily walking practice. She was not sorry when she was gently but firmly put back into bed; she still seemed to be off balance and the exercise made her head swim, she was still very weak, but the desire to burst into silly tears seemed to have gone for the present.

She lay in the darkness, eyes wide open, and gave herself up to thought. Leave everything in his hands? Yes, she was quite content to do that, but would it be wise? She might not be able to remember anything, but she was quite capable of recognising a domineering male when she saw one. Give him an inch and within an hour he'd be trampling all over her. Personally, she didn't mind being married to him in the least. If she must have a husband, he was just the sort she would have chosen.

Big and lazily dominating, he could be positively charming when he wished, his deep voice tender and gentle, his eyes gleaming with warmth and a wicked sensual humour. She would stand no chance at all, a doormat would have nothing on her, and what then?

She would be putty in those long sensitive hands. He would wreak havoc with her emotions. No, she told herself, it would be most unwise to be totally dependent, to allow herself to be moved about like a pawn on a chessboard. Just for a while, she thought, just for a very little while, she would leave things in his very capable hands. She hadn't any option really. He was in a position to organise and arrange, she wasn't.

Having arrived at this momentous decision, she closed her eyes and drifted away into a deep, dreamless sleep.

CHAPTER TWO

ATHOUGH she felt enormously better, Victoria found herself very reluctant to leave the hospital. The narrow, clean white world was very comforting and what was more important, it was the only world she knew. She felt rather like an inexperienced traveller setting forth into the unknown desert; she would very much like to take the last oasis with her or not go at all. She knew, of course, that she must go. It was now nearly four weeks since she had been admitted, her head wound had healed cleanly, the only thing to mark it was the growth of stubby, short hair along the line of the scar and a slight irregularity on the surface of her head. Her arm was still in plaster and would remain so for another four weeks at least. There was nothing to keep her here any longer except the fear of her unremembered past and her unknown future.

There was nothing more that the hospital could do for her; they had given her a breathing space, a time of grace. That was the period between Midsummer Day and another date when wild animals were not hunted, she mused. Her time of grace was up. Wryly, she wondered if the hunt would now be on. He had likened her to a wild animal, hadn't he?

Her mind filled with these gloomy thoughts, she tended to cling to her narrow bed and to the Sisters, as a child in the dark clings to a familiar toy. However, her feelings of fear had, over the past two days, given way to a sense of frustration and finally, to sheer temper.

She sat in a chair in a private room, fulminating silently while doctors, Matron and Sisters consulted with the man they said was her husband, about her future. Consulted with him? That was a laugh for a start! They fawned about his feet. Toadies, the whole lot of them!

The conversation was conducted mainly in English. Fortunately, Matron had trained in England at a well-known London hospital and the doctors, although far from fluent, were able to manage. Sister Maria Immaculata, as became a member of the nobility, spoke five languages and Sister Catalina had been taking lessons.

He wished that his wife should comprehend their arguments and decisions, therefore they would all speak his wife's native tongue. It seemed to Victoria that the only things they all had to say were 'Yes', 'No' and 'Thank you'.

He had decided that the time had come for her to leave the hospital, and the doctors agreed. Tomorrow would be ideal, not one dissenting voice was raised. Victoria was now quite steady on her legs and could walk, not far, but that would come, therefore she could be conveyed to her own home. *He* moved about the room exhibiting a charming brand of arrogance, rather like a well oiled steamroller. Any opposition was rolled out flat.

The stitches had been removed from the head wound and it was now healed, there was no pain in that area. Any subsequent X-rays, *he* would arrange, to give the minimum of inconvenience to the Señora. Her broken arm and wrist? *His* doctor would arrange for the removal of the offending, and by the look on his face offensive, plaster at the correct time. A mention by Sister Maria Immaculata of the patient's weak and nervous state brought forth first an annihilating glance and then a smile of such charm that the Sister gave way before it. Victoria decided that he was very well aware of the effect of that smile and she glared at him.

He felt sure that in the comfort of her own home,

supported by the love and care of her husband and surrounded, as she would be, by her devoted family and faithful, willing retainers, the Señora could not help but recover her equanimity. There would be faces, voices and objects which would without doubt stir her memory.

Little Dr Sanchez proved a minor stumbling block. The doctor was of the opinion that, as the Señora had shown such good progress in the hospital, another week might see the total recovery of her memory. In his opinion, this was a critical time. The Señora needed not so much hospital care as such, but a retreat in which to adjust to her traumatic experiences. There was a confirmatory nod from one of the other doctors, and Victoria gave a silent cheer. 'Lets see you get out of that one, my lad,' she said to herself, and waited for the annihilating glance or the charming smile to make an appearance, and was rather disappointed when he displayed neither. He merely ignored the remark as though it had never been made and continued a deeply serious discourse.

Of course, he would be eternally grateful for the care and attention, both medical and spiritual, which the Señora had received while in their care. He had nothing but praise for the whole hospital. He had noted, with some distress, when Matron had taken him on a tour of the premises—Matron received a smile and positively simpered—that the children's wards suffered from overcrowding. As a parent. . . .

Victoria jerked upright, unnoticed by the rest of the company who were literally hanging on his words. A parent? Did that mean that she . . .? Oh no! She couldn't have forgotten that! Meanwhile the deep imperturbable voice continued. . . , He was well aware of the need for extending facilities to cope with present-day needs regarding the care of children. He would give it his undivided attention. He knew that the hospital staff would realise that he and the Señora would wish to make some small gesture to indicate their gratitude.

Victoria ground her excellent white teeth in fury and suppressed with difficulty a desire to hit everyone very hard with her plastered arm. She could feel every copper-coloured hair on her head standing bolt upright as she surveyed the happy faces of the doctors and the Matron's fatuous smile of devotion. Even Sisters Maria Immaculata and Catalina, standing one on either side of her chair like archangels, exuded gratification at his mention of how deeply concious he was of his debt to their order.

Money was, obviously, no obstacle. Not only was he tall, dark and handsome, he was charming as well and filthy rich into the bargain. Then why on earth had he married her, Victoria? She had cost him a car, a big expensive one if she was any judge, and now he was willing to fund a new childen's ward and give a hefty donation to the order just to get her into his house without delay. Why?

Thoughts ran around in her head. Had she been wildly beautiful, exotic or elegant, she could have understood. But she wasn't any of those things. A smile curved her mouth. She didn't know if she was beautiful or just plain ugly, for neither of the Sisters had ever offered her a mirror. Perhaps mirrors weren't allowed. The lack of a reflection, however, could not convince her that she was anything but quite ordinary to look at. Certainly not worth an expensive car and a hospital ward. She gave up.

The charmingly arrogant steamroller rolled on, flattening out opposition like so many miles of macadam road. The Señora could leave today. He had brought with him garments suitable for travelling and the distance was not great enough to tire the Señora unduly. If she could be dressed . . .? The car was of the greatest comfort imaginable and his chauffeur was an old and trusted servant who had driven him many thousands of miles without mishap. Both car and chauffeur were at this very moment ready and waiting outside the hospital doors. It was nearly noon and the journey would take several hours; he wished the Señora to arrive home before dark. His own doctor would be within call should the Señora feel any ill effects. . . .

The Señora clenched her teeth and willy-nilly was led away to be dressed. A little of her temper evaporated at the sight of her clothes. A suit of pale green silk, with a pleated skirt and a sleeveless, boxy jacket, was teamed with a silk shirt in a darker green with wide, loose sleeves, evidently chosen with her plastered arm in mind. There was underwear, mere wisps of silk and lace which made Sister Catalina blush as she helped Victoria to put them on. The filmy tights were left in the case, they were too difficult to put on, so Victoria went barelegged, stuffing her feet into handmade Italian sandals, soft and delicate and as light as a feather.

Genuine tears of regret misted her eyes as she kissed the two nuns. They had been darlings to her and she wished that she didn't have to leave them. Sister Maria Immaculata smiled serenely but mentioned that in the mountains, below Candanchu, the order ran a small house of retreat. A word to the Reverend Mother would be all that was required if the *señora* . . .? Sister Catalina burst into volatile tears.

As Victoria collected together her belongings, she realised with a shock of dismay that after four visits and the hooh-hah of this morning, she still did not know her husband's name, so that he started with an advantage over her.

No fewer than three doctors, the Matron and the two nuns escorted them to the car. Victoria had made a bet with herself that it would be the biggest Mercedes sedan ever made, that it would be black and sparkle majestically in the sunlight. She won. It also had air-conditioning, electrically operated tinted windows and a chauffeur upholstered to match the interior. Sumptuous was the word for it.

The chauffeur made play with a travelling rug after he had carefully inserted her into the capacious rear of the car. He tucked it tenderly about her knees and let down a neat little footrest for her feet. His weatherworn, middle-aged face was kind and solicitous and he treated her as if she was something precious, smiling sympathetically as he disposed of her injured arm in a comfortable position. Under this sort of treatment, Victoria felt herself blossoming and wresting her attention from her husband and what she referred to mentally as his guard of honour, she smiled back at the chauffeur, murmuring that she was glad to see him.

'The Señor has told us of your sad condition, *señora*, the small awkwardnesses are bound to arise and it is better if we understand. Me, I am Carlos Ribiera, my wife, Pilar, is your cook.' Victoria smiled again and wished she could think of something to say, but the smile seemed to be enough. There was a final round of handshaking outside, then her husband seated himself beside her. Carlos slid behind the wheel and the car slipped away, leaving the guard of honour waving.

For a while, she watched the scenery. Down below them was a scorched yellow plain where Pamplona lay. The car skirted it for a while, then turned and headed up through green wooded foothills where jagged redbrown rocks reared on either side of the road. They were going towards the higher mountains. It all looked fresh and clean, which she thought strange. Always she had thought of Spain as hot, dry and brown.

Wrapped in a cocoon of silence, she watched the hills and the blue sky above her, trying desperately to think of something to say. There wasn't anything that wouldn't sound trite, banal or downright rude. She stole a glance at the imperious profile next to her and went ferreting around in her mind for an innocuous remark which she could make to this stranger whom she should know very well. In the dark places of her mind where her yesterdays were hiding, something stirred.

'Curtsey while you're thinking what to say,' she heard herself murmur. 'It saves time.'

'*Que pasa, querida?*' He turned instantly to regard her intently. His grey eyes had the most preposterous lashes, she thought—long and curling, and today his eyes mirrored sympathy and concern with, deep down, an expression of satisfaction. He quirked a dark eyebrow at her, a silent question.

'Curtsey while you're thinking what to say,' she repeated. 'That's what the Red Queen said to Alice in *Through the Looking Glass*. It's a book,' she explained carefully. 'I feel rather like Alice when she went through the looking glass and found herself in a topsy-turvey world where everything looked familiar but was very strange. There's one difference though, Alice was dreaming it all, but I'm not, am I?' Having started, she found no difficulty in going on. 'I'm sorry to have to remind you, but you haven't ever told me your name.'

A long-fingered, cool hand enclosed hers, which was warm and rather damp, and she felt the shift of his body as he slid his left arm around her shoulders, holding her firmly, drawing her to him. There was a moment of embarrassment when she felt as though she ought to pull away, but it retreated swiftly. The arm about her shoulders was warm and comforting. She liked it.

'My name is Rafael Sebastian Alvarez. It means nothing to you?'

Ruefully, she shook her head. 'Therefore,' he continued as one would to a child, 'you are Señora Alvarez.'

Well, at least she had a name! She tried it out silently. Victoria Alvarez—no, it wasn't familiar at all. She said it aloud. 'Victoria Alvarez.'

'That is logical, is it not? I, Rafael Sebastian Alvarez,

have an English wife whose name is Victoria. Therefore she must be Victoria Alvarez. No?'

He was laughing at her—treating her as though she had lost her intelligence when she lost her memory. She flashed him a sideways glance from under her lashes. She would not attempt to do battle yet, but later on, when she felt more herself.... A recent memory exploded in her mind.

'You said—that is, you told the doctors that you were a parent. Does this mean that I have a child? I've thought and thought about it,' she turned an agonised face to him. 'I couldn't forget my own child, could I? Surely nothing in the world would make me forget that?'

'No, *querida*, you have no child. How could you? We have been married for only three months.' He slanted a cool smile down at her. 'I referred to my daughter Isabel, who is eight years and whose mother died seven years ago. Isabel waits impatiently for your return.' Long fingers closed firmly over her clammy hand. 'She has a great affection for you and is greatly distressed that you have been hurt. It was partly for that reason that I removed you so speedily from the hospital. There is more than adequate care available to you in your own home and once Isabel has seen you and assured herself that her beloved Victoria has not disappeared for ever, then perhaps,' a wry smile curved his mouth, 'she will cease to behave like a watering pot and regain her former happiness.'

His arm tightened as he felt her slight withdrawal and he brought her back close to him, lifting her hand and examining her fingers almost absentmindedly. 'Yes, Victoria, I know that I speak as though Isabel and her happiness is my first concern and is all that is of importance to me, but this is not so. My concern in this matter has been for you. You have been hurt and your memory has gone.' His voice was deeply serious. 'It is natural that you should feel troubled, but as I have said before, in your own home, with your husband and family who love you, you will have a better chance of recovery than in a strange place among strangers, no matter how kind they may be. As for this idea of a retreat,' he shook her gently, 'it is nonsense! You are not the type to immure yourself in a house of women, so let me hear no more of it. I would not permit it!'

'But you are all strangers to me.' She sounded reasonable while she nobly stifled the rage engendered by his last remark behind a passive exterior.

He released her hand to put a finger under her chin, tipping her face up. He lowered his black head and very gently kissed her parted lips, a sweet, gentle kiss that demanded nothing and yet set her pulses racing. He raised his head and their eyes met for a long moment as she stared at him.

'That was to prove that we aren't strangers, I suppose?'

'Precisely, *mi mujer.*'

'Well,' she looked at him reflectively, 'I think your performance must be slipping. You failed to convince me.'

His mouth found hers again, but this time there was no gentleness, no sweetness, simply a hard demand against her lips, bruising them and unleashing a warmth inside her that shocked her. With a great effort, she neither pulled herself away nor yielded to the blatant demand. Outwardly she remained cool, although her heart was beating in an unruly fashion. At last he released her and she gave a gasp of outrage.

'Temper, temper!' he laughed down into her stormy eyes. 'What a pity that there is nothing for you to throw at me!'

Clutching the rags of her self-possession about her, Victoria wriggled away from him. 'I'm still not convinced,' she managed to say in a cool little voice. He merely regarded her with experienced eyes and drew her back forcibly against his shoulder. His hand came up to press her head down on to his chest.

'Go to sleep, *querida*. This part of the journey is very boring. Rest for a while and then we shall have some refreshment. Pilar has packed us a basket and there is coffee as well. We will find a pleasant spot and have a picnic.'

She relaxed against him. Just at present she did not feel capable of coping with him, especially in his present mood. Later, of course, when she was less tired, when her vitality was not at such a low ebb, she would. . . . Her eyelids drooped; she would. . . . She never did tell herself what she would do later on when she was quite well, for her head slid heavily down to rest somewhere near his breast pocket. She felt the warmth of his body under her cheek and slept peacefully for nearly an hour.

She awakened to find the car pulled off the road. Sleepily, she enquired if they had arrived.

'No, Victoria. This is a good place to stop for some refreshment. We have another hour's journeying yet. It is not the distance, you understand? It is the road. It is not a good road.'

'I know,' she responded, still only half awake. 'Potholes, the biggest potholes in Europe.' She yawned and put up a hand to push back a lock of hair that fell forward over her forehead. Pulling herself upright, she surveyed her rumpled green silk ruefully. 'I must look a mess.'

From a side pocket of the car, he produced a small mirror. 'See for yourself.'

She accepted the mirror eagerly and stared at her reflection. Was this really her? Large green-flecked hazel eyes stared back at her out of a pale face. A small straight nose—she touched it and her reflection copied the gesture. Her fingers slid down to her mouth. Too wide for beauty and the short upper lip didn't help, she told herself. Then her finger went down to a firm small chin.

It was as she thought; she was no beauty, only passably good-looking. Her eyes were rather nice, she decided, fringed as they were with thick dark lashes, and her eyebrows were dark as well, for which she was thankful. She didn't think she would have liked eyebrows that matched her copper-coloured hair, or red eyelashes either. She was just deciding that her triangular face reminded her of a cat when his voice broke in on her thoughts.

'I have heard you say that before—about the potholes. You see, something comes back even if you do not realise it. Of course,' he continued sarcastically, 'I may regret the passing of this quiet, compliant version of my wife, but even if you regain all of your former belligerence, I shall not complain.'

'What on earth do you mean?' she glared at him.

'Ah, *querida*, I forget that you have forgotten. Here we have been travelling together for several hours and not once have you argued with me, nor have you defied me. Neither have you thrown anything at my head!'

'Was it like that?' a flush of embarrassment rose in her cheeks.

'*Seguro*, certainly. It was just like that! Not what you would call a peaceful life,' he slanted a wicked glance down at her. 'There were compensations, of course, and it was never dull.'

Before Victoria could reply, Carlos appeared with a small hamper containing Thermos flasks and beakers. There was a plastic box containing sandwiches, a jar of olives, slices of delicious-looking cake and several large peaches and pears. Deftly, Carlos poured coffee for them before going with his own share of the food to sit under a stunted tree.

Victoria thought that it was a beautiful place for a

picnic and said so to this stranger whom she should know very well. 'It's so green and peaceful, and those mountains in the distance are quite awe-inspiring.'

'It is Navarre.' It was a simple statement.

'You love it, don't you?' Her voice was almost a whisper.

He turned his head to look at her. 'I am a Navarese. We think that this is the most beautiful part of Spain, of the whole world. If possible, we try never to leave it. Once it was a kingdom, small but proud. Do you recall Charlemagne's battle in the pass of Roncevalles? Roland and Oliver and a horn? A few Christian knights against the Moorish hordes? That was all a fantasy of the old French chroniclers.' He snorted disdainfully. 'The Moors never penetrated this far north. Charlemagne's battle was Christian looters against the Navarese. Our legends say that on the way back to France, Charlemagne and his men looted Pamplona, so the Navarese crept up by night and ambushed the Christian army in the pass. Charlemagne retreated from there very quickly.' He turned his head to look at her, his face harsh. 'Yes, *querida*, I love Navarre. It is small, it lacks magnificence except in its mountains, we have no particular sort of cooking or wine, no grand palaces, but to me it is home and always will be. Do you know that when the tourists come, sometimes they find not one frontier barricade but two? After they have passed through the Spanish Customs, those who take a less popular route sometimes find another barrier across the road. They stop and are taken to a building or perhaps only a table under a tree, and a group of solemn men inspect their passports once again and welcome them to the kingdom of Navarre.' He chuckled. 'It is a little game they play. The Spanish police leave us alone to our harmless fun, otherwise rocks might topple from mountains upon unwary heads.'

The tension had sloughed from her like a dead skin

and she laughed delightedly. 'Sister Catalina comes from
Lecumberi—that's in Navarre, isn't it? You disappointed her!' He raised one eyebrow. 'She wanted me to
possess a fluffy pink bedjacket. To her it's the height of
luxury. When you brought my things, there was no bedjacket at all, much less a pink fluffy one. I'm glad in a
way, I once had a pink dress . . .' She stopped suddenly,
the laughter dying from her eyes.

'And what of this pink dress?' he prompted casually.

Victoria shook her head. 'I don't know, just that
I had one. It was a very bright pink and I hated
it!'

'Forget it.' His face had become grim. 'So many
things, so much that you have forgotten, but you remember a pink dress with displeasure.' He looked up at
the sky. 'I think it is time we resumed our journey. The
hottest part of the day is now over and we shall travel
in more comfort.' As if in answer to a signal, Carlos
came, collecting beakers and plates to stow away in the
hamper. Within a few minutes the car was back on the
road, a road that wound ever deeper into the foothills
of the mountains.

Her inability to remember any more about the pink
dress worried Victoria. She could see it so very plainly
in her mind's eye, the frill around the neck, the puff
sleeves, even the sash of a slightly darker pink, but
nothing else. She frowned with effort, but her mind
remained a blank.

'Do not worry yourself, *querida*. You are sitting there
like a little cat, ready to spring. You have remembered
something more, surely that is a step in the right direction? There is no need for these unhappy looks. The day
is beautiful, you do not have any pain and you are going
home. You should be happy. You were happy before
you thought of this stupid pink dress.'

Victoria felt a mild surprise. Yes, she had been
happy, listening to his tales of Navarre, eating the peach

which he had peeled for her. She had felt as if she hadn't a care in the world. 'I was happy, wasn't I?' she sought assurance.

'Yes, you were.' He sounded quite definite about it.

CHAPTER THREE

At about half past three the car turned off the road and
ran between the tall pillars of high iron gates. Each pillar
was topped with a somewhat bloodthirsty effigy of an
eagle in the act of rending the carcase of some animal to
pieces. The savage totems did very little to calm
Victoria's nerves or increase her sense of 'coming home'.
Her nerves had been jangling for the last half hour,
during which time the terrain had become wilder and
more mountainous.

During the last ten minutes they had passed through
a small village, but there was little sign of life. The shuttered windows turned blind eyes to the street from
behind their iron grilles. A large cat, sunning itself in a
window box of geraniums, blinked oblique green eyes
as the car went past. The little grey stone church with
its squat tower stood silent in the bright sunlight.
Everybody must be having a siesta, Victoria thought.

Perhaps everybody at 'home' was having a siesta as
well. She had a sudden wild desire to find herself a nice
dark hole, crawl into it and pull it in on top of herself.
She didn't want strange, curious eyes looking at her
from faces she did not know, could not remember. She
gnawed her bottom lip and felt a film of perspiration
bedew her body.

A soft laugh came from the man beside her. 'You
look like a Christian about to be thrown to the lions,
pequeña. Stop worrying—nobody is going to eat you, I
promise.'

The house came in sight and her heart sank further.
This was 'home'? This grim, grey, tower-like building?
She stared aghast at the enormous iron-studded door,

at the windowless façade—unless you could call arrow slits windows; there were lots of those, and there was also another vicious-looking stone eagle carved in a niche above the door. Victoria shuddered.

Carlos brought the car smoothly to a halt in front of three wide, shallow steps in front of the door. With the ease of long practice, he was out of the car and holding the door open for her before she realised that they had stopped. Her husband descended more leisurely and came to give her his hand on to the gravel sweep of the drive. Her legs had become rubbery again so that she was forced to steady herself against the side of the car. He let loose with a short burst of Spanish which was totally incomprehensible to her, although she strongly suspected that it was bad language, and picked her up bodily, carrying her up the steps and in through the door which, by some conjuring trick, opened just as he reached it. Victoria found herself lowered to her feet and looked around in a bewildered way. She stood blinking while her eyes adjusted to the change from bright sunlight to this rather gloomy interior.

She was in an enormous square room with a high raftered ceiling. The unrendered walls were decorated here and there with a selection of warlike implements and there were several tapestries, large ones hung about covering portions of the massive stones of the walls. Light filtered in through the slit-like windows high in the walls and illuminated an enormous fireplace, large enough to roast an ox whole. This seemed to occupy all of one wall. A number of large, aged wooden chests were ranged around the walls, interspersed with some uncomfortable-looking carved oak chairs, all highly polished and shining blackly, while just inside the great door stood a table, the top of which gleamed like black silk, reflecting the copper bowl which stood on it.

Several large carpets managed to look like small islands of colour in an ocean of grey flagstones, and

Victoria thought that she had never seen such an uncomfortable room in her life. She took another look
around and cheered up considerably. This must serve as
some sort of an entrance hall, it was obviously not lived
in. In the gloom, she picked out more highly polished
copper bowls and jugs together with some massive pieces
of blue and white porcelain standing about on the
polished chests; they should have softened the stark
appearance of the room, but instead they merely served
to emphasise the entire lack of comfort.

Further inspection was interrupted. One of the two
doors leading off from this hall was flung open to disclose
an enormous female who bore down on them, a stream
of Spanish falling from her lips meanwhile. Her ample
bosom heaved with emotion, tears were pouring down
her face and the vast white apron that covered her long
black dress billowed like the sails of a racing yacht.

Victoria found herself enveloped in a massive em-
brace, brawny arms enfolded her while the torrent of
words continued unchecked, pouring over her head.
Without understanding more than a word here and
there, she was conscious of being petted, sympathised
with, scolded and exclaimed over all at once and at some
length.

'Pilar,' her husband explained, sounding amused. 'The
wife of Carlos and our much valued cook. She says that
you are too thin, that you were wicked to cause us all so
much distress, that her heart breaks to see how you have
suffered, that she cried like a little child when news came
that you had been found but now that you are at home
once more, she will care for you and you will be so
happy, contented and fat that you will never wish to
leave us again.'

Impulsively, Victoria gathered into her arms as
much of Pilar's person as she could hold, which wasn't
much, and hugged it, raising herself on tiptoe to
plant a soft kiss on a cheek as rosy as a well ripened

apple, and as round.

'Thank you, Pilar—oh, thank you' Her voice broke on the edge of tears while a tide of relief spread through her whole being. She had found a friend, somebody who reminded her of someone else equally uninhibited, whose emotions, unrestrained, had also poured out in a warm, soothing flow. She couldn't remember who it had been; that was hidden behind the dark curtain that cut off her yesterdays.

Pilar laughed, a fat hearty laugh, and strode off, back through the door that evidently led to the kitchen regions, but before she reached it, a cool detached voice cut like a knife through the hall.

'You must forgive her, Victoria. It is always the same with these peasants. Any little thing and they become emotional. That is the word, no?'

Victoria swung round as if she had been stung, all the warmth engendered by Pilar's tempestuous welcome dissipated, leaving her cold and empty.

The girl advanced with an elegant, graceful step. No, not a girl, decided Victoria, a woman, as elegant and graceful as her mode of walking. Nothing could have been more chic than the simple cream linen dress which skimmed a figure beyond compare. The long slender neck looked almost too frail to support the small proud head with its chignon of glossy, raven black hair. The face was a smooth, unlined, perfect oval; ivory-skinned with a delicate flush of pink in the cheeks. Magnificent black eyes held a slumbrous glow beneath heavy lids fringed with long silky lashes and a red mouth curved enticingly, disclosing perfect teeth.

'Inez,' Rafael whispered in her ear. His arm was heavy about her shoulders and she was grateful for its weight and warmth, for, despite the welcoming smile, Inez brought with her a cold remoteness. It was not obvious, Rafael did not seem to notice it, but Victoria felt it, chill and bitter. Nothing as positive as hostility, but it was

there in the dark eyes, even in the red curve of the
mouth. Victoria took the gracefully extended hand, a
smooth, cool cheek touched hers and a thread of perfume, heavy and exotic, assailed her nostrils. Inez drew
back.

'Yes, Pilar was right.' It might have been imagination
but there seemed to Victoria to be satisfaction in the
dulcet tones. 'You are much thinner, almost scraggy. Is
that the right word?' She looked over Victoria's head,
speaking to Rafael. 'Abuela and Isabel are waiting in
the *sala*. Do come at once. Isabel heard the car arrive
and I've had the greatest difficulty since; she wished to
come running out here in a very hoydenish fashion.'

The *sala* came as a pleasant surprise. Evidently the
entrance hall was part of the original building, some
kind of fortress, thought Victoria. Behind it, much later,
somebody had added a gracious, comfortable house
with tall, wide windows, mellow panelling and glowing
wooden floors. She breathed a sigh of relief. She could
not have lived, she told herself, in the cold austerity of a
mediaeval castle, but here there was warmth and light.
Comfortable-looking chairs were upholstered in rich
tapestry, the furniture, although heavy, glowed with the
rosy brown of mahogany, not black oak. The walls,
washed white, were hung with pictures and portraits in
curly gold frames and the windows gave a wide view of
the sunlit slopes of the foothills.

Seated primly in a tapestry-covered chair, her small
feet on a matching footstool, was an old lady. Silver
hair gleamed dully through the fine lace of a black
mantilla. The child beside her on another stool raised a
piquant little face under a mop of glossy black curls.

'Victoria!' she cried, and rising, flung herself across
the room in an awkward shambling gait. Gaining her
objective, which was apparently to clasp Victoria's knees
in a grip of iron, the child looked up into the face above
her enquiringly.

Without conscious thought, Victoria dropped on to her knees and enfolded the small eager body in her arms, holding the child close against her, partly to conceal the piteous tears occasioned by the cruel-looking steel brace on the child's leg.

'Isabel,' she whispered. 'Oh dear!' as she caught sight of the child's tears. 'Now don't let us both weep, we'll make a puddle on the floor.'

'Oh, Victoria!' Satisfaction glowed on Isabel's face. 'You *do* remember me! Tia Inez said that we would all be strangers to you, that you wouldn't know any of us. But I knew you'd remember me. You do, don't you?'

Over the black, glossy little head, Victoria's eyes met Rafael's. As plainly as if he had spoken, she felt the plea in his dark grey eyes.

'How could I forget you, my darling?' The lump in her throat made the words husky and lifting a hand, she brushed away the tears from her cheeks. 'Of course I remember you,' she asserted sturdily. 'You're quite unforgettable! The taut little body in her arms softened with relief and with a sunny smile the child turned and limped to her father, who picked her up, setting her on his shoulder. She maintained her balance by clutching a handful of his hair, thereby destroying his impeccable appearance and rendering him, in his wife's eyes at least, much more human.

A very few steps took her to stand before the old lady. 'Abuela?' she said softly. Old eyes surveyed her sharply for several seconds.

'So, child, you have come back to us.' The old voice was surprisingly strong and deep. She motioned to the footstool so recently vacated by Isabel. 'Sit here for a moment and let me look at you. Hm! As Inez says, you are thinner. That is to be expected, of course. One cannot throw oneself about the highway, sustaining various serious injuries, and emerge looking as before. And you remember nothing?' Victoria shook her head.

'A few impressions only. A pink dress I hated, somebody like Pilar, with her exuberance; perhaps it was Pilar, I don't know. Apart from that, nothing.'

'A pink dress!' The old lady snorted. 'No wonder you hated it. I cannot think of any colour more unbecoming to you! You dealt very well with the child, you did not hurt her—but then you have always been kind. Of this amnesia we will speak no more. I feel sure that it will pass, for you are young, you will recover. Meanwhile, when the little difficulties arise, you shall come come to me—to me, child or to your husband.'

There seemed to be an oblique warning in Abuela's voice; certainly the old blue-veined hand with its thin, beringed fingers tightened on hers fractionally as she spoke. The old lady continued, 'Nevertheless, we have missed you and it is good to have you back with us. There has been no afternoon tea which I so much enjoyed sharing with you and there has been very little laughter about the house. *Mi nieto*, my grandson, has been like a bear with a headache and Isabel has watered her milk with her tears constantly since you disappeared. And me, I am old, and as are all old people, I am selfish. I have not been so comfortable without you.' Victoria managed a small smile as Abuela looked at her sternly. 'For myself, I do not think this lack of memory is of any consequence. When you came here a year ago, you did not know us, but you learned to love us. What you did once, you can do again.'

Inez interrupted. 'Pilar is preparing tea. It is a drink to which you are addicted, are you not?' The words were innocuous, but Victoria felt as though she had been accused of smoking opium. She took refuge in flippancy.

'I'd die without it,' she laughed. 'Abuela is an addict as well, so I hope Pilar makes a big pot.'

'For you, *querida*, there will be tea, but upstairs in your room where you are going now, to rest.' A com-

mand from the lord and master, Victoria thought re-
belliously, but he was correct, of course. She had
worried herself about meeting these people, and now it
was over and it hadn't been half the ordeal which her
imagination had made it. She wasn't tired, she was limp
with relief. Inez threw another pointed little dart.

'But of course, Rafael. See, her face is quite white
and there are dark circles under her eyes.'

So! thought Victoria. First I'm skinny, then I'm a drug
addict, and now I'm a hag! She glared at Rafael, willing
herself to sit up very straight on the footstool. It made
no difference. His arms scooped her up as if she was of
no more weight than Isabel. She was carried up the wide
shallow stairs, along a corridor, and deposited on her
feet, by a door.

'This, *querida*, is our bedroom,' he said conversa-
tionally. 'It is, as you see, most convenient.' He flung
open the door and gestured. 'Here, through this door, is
your dressing room, and beyond it your bathroom. Over
here,' he pointed to a door on the opposite wall, 'is my
dressing room and shower.'

Victoria remained riveted by the bedroom door, her
eyes fixed on the bed. It was a very large bed and it
seemed to have an hypnotic effect on her. She hardly
spared a glance for the rest of the room, charming
though it was with a cream carpet, gold upholstered
chairs and gold curtains. She swallowed convulsively.

'We sleep here? You sleep here?' Colour washed over
her pale face.

'But of course. I am your husband, am I not? Where
else would I sleep but with my wife? Ah, I see what it is.
You still think of me as a stranger—but I am not a
stranger, I am your husband. For three months we have
occupied this bed together, most pleasurably,' he slanted
a cool glance down at her, 'and I refuse, absolutely, to
re-start our married life in a different fashion. No,
Victoria, your memory may be faulty, but mine is not,

so that I have many extremely pleasant recollections of nights we have spent together in this bed and also of the pleasure which was, I assure you, mutual. I refuse to forgo this simply because you do not remember.'

Victoria continued to look at him with a dazed, glassy look in her eyes. How could he talk about such intimate things in such a matter-of-fact fashion? Speaking of pleasurable nights as if he was discussing a dinner he'd eaten! As if they were a long time married couple to whom such things were an integral part of life and could therefore be discussed without embarrassment. But they had been married for three months, she reminded herself, and a lot could happen in three months. She forced a light laugh and wrinkled her nose at him.

'It's the bed—it looks so huge. I'd just become used to the narrow ones in hospital. I'd be lost in this one alone.'

'The head and footboards are very old,' he explained. 'The rest, however, is new and the mattress was specially made. You always found it very comfortable.' He was by her side, turning her towards him, his eyes looking into hers with a challenge. There was a moment's immobility, then with a sound very like a groan he lowered his black head and his mouth found hers.

A wicked mouth, Victoria decided. A wicked, experienced mouth—and after that she thought very little at all, being too busy attempting to crush down several very strong emotions—emotions which if she gave way to them would make her body go quite limp, might even send her hand up to hold down that black head so that his mouth would never leave hers. She failed in this laudable attempt, failed miserably, observing in a detached sort of way that she was behaving in a deplorable manner. Lovemaking in the afternoon, and in a very uninhibited way! Rafael's hands caressed the curve of her hips, drawing her closer, his mouth slid down the line of her throat and across to a point just behind her ear which he bit gently.

'*Te quiero, amada,*' she heard his whisper in her ear, the tickle of his breath sending little shivers down her spine. She sighed as his hand found her breast and she drew his head down to hers.

'Somebody might come,' she whispered against his lips.

'Then they can go away again,' he answered hardily.

'You said I must rest.' She tried, not very hard, to pull away from him.

'So I did!' Grey eyes danced with laughter. 'Perhaps I wished to satisfy myself that all was as it was before.'

'And is it?' Her voice was warm and rather breathless.

'*Si, mi mujer,* and just as eminently satisfactory, but there are some small things that need attention.' His fingers flicked Sister Catalina's plaits. 'Your hair, braided so, makes you look not much older than Isabel, and I have no wish to appear as an elderly satyr ravishing a child—although,' contemplatively, 'your response is far from childlike.'

'And I don't think you qualify for the title of "elderly satyr".' Her fingers stroked the back of his head. 'How old are you?'

'I have thirty-five years, *querida*, and look every one of them. Possibly the result of a misspent youth.'

Victoria heard herself giggle. 'Details, please, of this misspent youth.'

'Not so much misspent as wasted.' His mouth found hers again and warm weakness flooded through her.

Raising his head, he growled something in Spanish. Curses, that was what it sounded like, and she found herself dumped unceremoniously on the bed. Away from the warmth of his arms and body she felt cold and desolate, and a tear slid slowly down her cheek.

'Victoria,' he scowled at her, 'don't look at me so—do you not understand? I am not to be trusted.'

From the pillow, she smiled up at him. 'I know,' she said it softly. 'As soon as I saw you in the hospital, I said to myself, 'Here is a man who shouldn't be trusted. . . .' The rest of this worthy speech was lost against his mouth, against the warmth and hard demand of his body, lost in the caress of his hands. She closed her eyes as his lips became tender, sweet, coaxing and coercing, demanding a response that came from her as naturally as breathing.

Some time later she opened her eyes drowsily and examined the bedside clock unbelievingly. Two hours! Suspiciously, she picked up the little clock and turned it in her fingers. Two fat cupids held the dial in a garland of porcelain roses; it was a pretty thing, but was it going? She shook it gently and held it to her ear. The soft, regular tick reassured her. It was going and presumably telling the truth; she had slept for two hours and she felt wonderful and extremely hungry.

Remembering back to the morning, she recalled the hurried breakfast of coffee and a roll, then there had been the picnic lunch, but sandwiches, no matter how delicious, didn't have the same sustaining qualities as a nice thick steak. Thinking of a steak made her face grow wistful—about an inch thick, smothered with mushrooms; how long would it be before dinner?

Rafael came in silently, followed by a young girl, evidently a maid.

'I've brought Maria for you,' he smiled down at her in an absentminded way and Victoria, recalling her somewhat—no, not somewhat, her very abandoned behaviour earlier, felt hot colour sweeping over her face.

His mouth curved into a smile again, although his tone was prosaic. 'Maria will help you to bathe and dress for dinner. Tomorrow, Pilar is sending down to the village for her niece to come and help with Maria's work so that you may have her services more frequently. Until you can manage for yourself, that is. Before your accident, you were sturdily independent, refusing a maid.'

'I don't want one now,' she told him. 'Well, not all the time, just while it's awkward. After that, I can manage very well by myself.'

He nodded, the subject evidently boring him. 'As you wish *señora*, but go with Maria now. When you are dressed I will take you downstairs. We must stop and say goodnight to Isabel, who has had her supper and is now getting ready for bed, so there is no time to be lost. Abuela tells me that from the noise in the kitchen, Pilar is excelling herself, and we must not keep her food waiting.' He crossed to his own dressing room and paused with his hand on the door. 'Twenty minutes, Victoria, is that enough time for you?'

She gulped and slid out of the bed, bundling herself into the green velvet robe and joining Maria in the bathroom. Ten minutes later she sat in her slip at the dressing table while Maria brushed her hair. Several more minutes were wasted while they tried to achieve a smooth chignon with hair that clung obstinately to the brush and to their fingers as if it had a life of its own. Finally defeated, they agreed that it would look quite becoming if it was tied back with a chiffon scarf. Already Maria had laid out on the bed a gold-embroidered green silk caftan. This had been selected for the ease with which it could be put on and for the loose, long sleeves which would hide the plaster on her arm. Now Maria was sent scurrying to find a scarf to match it.

Victoria applied the minimum of make-up and stuffed her feet into gold sandals. A clean handkerchief, a spray of perfume and she surveyed the results of their labours in a full-length mirror and felt mildly pleased. Yes, it would do. She lacked elegance, but one could hardly be elegant with hair tired back with a scarf and hanging down one's back, but the overall effect was quite good. She smiled her thanks at Maria as Rafael came out of his dressing room looking suave and very man-of-the-

worldly in a beautiful, black jacket over a white shirt
that had ruffles down the front. In black trousers, his
legs looked even longer.

Isabel was bundling herself into bed when they
entered her bedroom. Open on the bed in a very con-
spicuous position was a story book and there was a
silent plea in the little girl's eyes.

Obedient to the unspoken request, Victoria seated
herself on the bed and began to read aloud, going slowly
so that the child could query any English words that
were unfamiliar to her. Rafael lounged against the wall
watching them and occasionally glancing at his watch.
When the story was finished, Victoria kissed the little
girl and promised a morning spent playing in the
garden, unless Papa had other plans in mind.

Going down the stairs she worried aloud about her
hair. 'Maria and I tried for ages to get it up tidily, but
we failed miserably. It's not too untidy, is it?' And then
she chided herself for asking such a question of a man.

His arm tightened about her waist. 'Leave it like that,
I prefer it so.'

'But. . . .'

Rafael halted at the bottom of the stairs and turned
her to face him. 'Why do you worry yourself about other
people's opinions? Isabel likes you whatever you wear
or however you have done your hair. She and I, we are
the only ones you need to please as far as your appearance goes.'

Seating herself beside Abuela in the *sala* for a pre-
dinner sherry, Victoria meekly accepted the one he
poured for her. 'Sweet,' he said. 'You do not care for dry
wines. Abuela and Inez, they have more of a palate,
Inez especially. She is a very good judge of wine.'

'A compliment at last!' Inez had entered while he was
speaking. 'Is it only for my palate that you appreciate
me?'

'Of course not.' He was smoothly polite, but Victoria

noticed that he eyed Inez with appreciation. She was certainly worth looking at. Her glossy black hair was drawn back into just the smooth chignon which Victoria and Maria had tried to achieve without success. Moreover, the chignon was decorated with a tortoiseshell comb, the high back of which was pierced and fretted so that it looked like golden lace. Her face was made up perfectly, the eyes skilfully shadowed so that they looked like enormous black pools. The dress she was wearing shrieked 'Paris' in its utter simplicity of black silk. Victoria, still smouldering over her despised sweet sherry, thought cattily that the dress exposed more of Inez than a small family dinner warranted and the fine black lace shawl she was wearing did more to draw attention to ivory shoulders and bosom than to conceal anything.

By this time, Rafael and Inez had wandered away to a window where they stood looking out on to the rapidly darkening landscape and talking in swift, sibilant Spanish. Victoria heard her husband's deep amused laugh and saw Inez's long, slender hand, ringless, and the nails tinted to a deep pink, placed possessively on his arm.

She gritted her teeth firmly but silently and with a gentle smile plastered on her lips, helped herself to another glass of the despised sweet sherry and listened to Abuela's exposition on the qualities desirable in a really good wine—dry, of course!

Pilar had truly excelled herself. There were fresh prawns in a delicious, tangy sauce, little fish whose sweet flesh melted in the mouth, steaks of noble proportions with mushrooms and tiny peas and a compote of fresh fruit with lashings of fresh cream. Abuela ate heartily in the manner of old people. 'My last great enjoyment,' she told Victoria. 'As one grows older, the things that one can enjoy grow fewer, but even at the end one still has pleasure in a fine wine and good food.

Age cannot spoil them!'

Inez merely picked at a little fish and green salad. Ruefully laughing, she allowed her half filled plate to be removed by Carlos, who had shed his chauffeur's uniform and had donned in its place a black jacket with winking silver buttons and striped trousers.

'I shall be in Pilar's bad books, I fear,' Inez smiled. 'I am certain that she looks at the plates as they go back to the kitchen. Either that or Maria tells her who is not eating much.' She sighed gently. 'Pilar is so very touchy. I think sometimes that she only likes people if they eat like horses.'

Victoria speared her last piece of steak viciously. So! Not only was she a skinny, drug-addicted hag, now she was a greedy pig! She smiled sweetly across the table at anybody who cared to be looking and remarked in dulcet tones that everybody had remarked how thin she was, so she was building herself up—and besides, she gave her husband a pointed look, the unaccustomed activity of her first day out of hospital had made her quite dreadfully hungry. But, she thought, whoever it was that said 'Better a dinner of herbs where love is' knew what he was talking about! She would have infinitely preferred bread and cheese if she could have eaten it without having to suffer these pricking little darts from dear Inez. Not that she wasn't capable of hurling a few darts herself. She was! But somehow, she could not bring herself to mention the tendency of Latins to get fat and the necessity therefore for dieting.

These inner thoughts caused her eyes to widen and darken and her mouth drooped a little, so that she looked, although she did not know it, like a wistful kitten. Rafael glanced at her and tossed his napkin aside. 'We will have coffee in the *sala*,' he announced.

Victoria sighed with relief. The delicious fruit compote had turned to dust and ashes in her mouth. Abuela raised her eyes in a silent question and, correctly interpreting the barely visible gesture of her grandson's head, turned sharp, dark eyes upon his wife, who was visibly sagging in her tall ladderbacked chair.

'That will be very pleasant, *nieto*. In my back is a small pain, hardly worth the mention at the moment, but I am sure that I shall be more comfortable in the *sala*. We all will. A cushion at my back and a stool for my feet, and for Victoria, a soft chair.' She rose and went to the door, her cane tapping on the polished floor. 'No, save your arm for your wife,' she waved aside Rafael's proffered hand. 'The child is weary, I am merely old!'

Victoria denied stoutly that she needed any help. 'It's my head and arm that were damaged,' she smiled at Abuela. 'There's nothing wrong with my legs.'

The old lady seated herself in the tapestry chair in which Victoria had first seen her, and which seemed to be her favourite. When the cushion at her back had been adjusted to her satisfaction, she set her feet on the footstool and gave Victoria a look of amusement.

'Your last remark, child, that there was nothing wrong with your legs. How times have changed! I can just recall the days when a Spanish lady did not have legs. They all pretended that their feet sprouted from the bottom of their skirts.' She sighed, almost with regret. 'Two world wars, a revolution in Spain and more than sixty years have helped to end part of that attitude, although I believe that Spain is still considered somewhat backward in these matters. There is a society, I believe, in America and also in Europe, which calls itself "Women's Lib".' Her mouth shaped the words distastefully. 'Have you heard of them, Victoria?'

Victoria had, and said so. 'It's partly a serious movement, at least it is in England,' she explained. 'Of course, it has the usual lunatic fringe which gains most of the press coverage and notoriety, but the really serious women do have some very sensible aims.'

Rafael cocked a disbelieving eyebrow at her. 'Such as?' he queried.

Victoria blushed and admitted that she couldn't bring any to mind at the moment. 'But,' she faced him defiantly, 'I'm sure that these serious aims exist!'

Abuela patted her hand. 'Do not enter into an argument with that one,' she advised dryly. 'Tell me instead what it was like, this hospital where you have been.'

Rafael looked at his grandmother with amusement. 'What could Victoria tell you about the hospital that I cannot? She was in it for several weeks, but I think she saw no more than one room, whereas I had a conducted tour of the buildings.'

'The one room I saw was very nice,' Victoria spared him a scathing glance, 'and as soon as I'm quite well again and this plaster is off, I'd like to go back and thank everyone for being so kind to me.'

During this speech Abuela, with the ease of old age, dozed in her chair. When Victoria's voice ceased, she opened her eyes and agreed that it would be a kindly gesture. 'If I feel well enough, I shall accompany you,' she said firmly. 'I look forward to the expedition.' She then decided that she would retire. 'No, I will not have any coffee. Sancha,' she turned to Victoria, 'she is my maid; she will be waiting for me with something more soothing to drink. I shall dislike it intensely.' The old lady rose from her chair. 'I always do dislike Sancha's bedtime drinks, so I wash away the taste with a glass of my grandson's good wine which I find ensures me a good night's sleep. Goodnight, child.' She stopped by the couch and Victoria felt an old hand gently touch her hair.

Victoria scrambled to her feet and reached up to kiss the wrinkled cheek, wondering meanwhile where were all the small, dark people whom she had always believed inhabited Spain. Rafael was tall, about six foot, she thought; Inez was also well above average height and

Abuela had once been a tall woman. Even now, stooped with age, she towered above Victoria's five foot two inches.

There were so many things that she would have to find out, and she sighed as Rafael escorted his grandmother up the stairs. Firstly, she wanted to know exactly who Inez was; nobody had explained that to her. Her brow wrinkled in thought as she tried to remember if anybody had said anything that might give her a clue and decided that they hadn't. Abuela called Inez, 'Inez,' not 'nieta', so there was no help from that quarter. Isabel hadn't mentioned Inez and Rafael's whispering of the name had been no introduction. Didn't they realise, she thought irritably, that it was very awkward not knowing who people were?

'Buenas noches,' she said halfheartedly as she watched her husband escort his grandmother upstairs. Turning again to the sala, she found Pilar at her elbow, chattering soft Spanish queries. 'It was a beautiful meal,' Victoria's face crinkled with pleasure, 'and I was so hungry.' This was spoken in English, but it must have got through, for Pilar beamed and flooded her with words. She felt Rafael's hand on her shoulder.

'Pilar says that hunger is a fine sauce and that if you have hunger, you must be well _gain.' There was a swift exchange of Spanish and Pilar departed for the nether regions, smiling broadly and doubtless intent upon harrying her minions to plan and produce further mouthwatering and satisfying meals.

'And for you, querida, there will be no coffee.' Rafael gave a little tug to the mane of coppery hair hanging down his wife's back. 'Pilar has sent Maria to our room to help you to undress and into bed. There is also waiting for you a glass of hot milk which you must drink.'

Victoria felt a momentary desire to insist that there was nothing wrong with her, that she wanted some coffee and that it was too early to go to bed, but she found herself stifling a yawn of mammoth proportions.

'You see, *querida*, it is as I say. You are tired, so in this small matter, you will not defy me, hmm?' Swiftly he picked her up and carried her upstairs, setting her on her feet just within the bedroom door. She felt his mouth warm against her temple. 'Two cups of coffee, one cigarette, and I shall join you. Shall you be asleep by then?'

'Of course not,' she said sturdily. 'I wish you wouldn't keep treating me as if I was an invalid. I could have walked up those stairs quite easily, there was no need for you to carry me. I told you earlier, there's nothing wrong with my legs.'

'No, Victoria,' he was nearly laughing. 'They are like the rest of your small person, quite charming!'

A most aggravating man, she decided when later she lay in bed. Either he was laying down the law with a firm hand or laughing at her. On the whole, she thought sleepily, she could enjoy being married if it wasn't for Inez. Ah well, every garden of Eden had its serpent. She lay in bed, her sleepy mind making fuzzy plans. As soon as Rafael came, she would find out just who Inez was, and as soon as she felt a little stronger, more able to hold her own, she would ... she would.... Victoria drifted off to sleep with a small smile on her face.

CHAPTER FOUR

SHE woke to bright sunshine and a fresh warm breeze blowing through the open windows, stirring the heavy, gold curtains and setting the lighter net ones dancing. Delightedly, Victoria scrambled out of bed and stood close to the window. Lovely day, she thought inhaling lungsful of the warm, scented air. She was alone in the bedroom and there was no sound from Rafael's dressing-room. The little bedroom clock said half past seven, so if she hurried, she could join him for breakfast. Last night he had said that he breakfasted early and she was hungry again. She gathered up a robe and some fresh underwear from a drawer in the dressing chest and headed for the bathroom.

With a little ingenuity, and surely she was capable of that, she could manage on her own. There was no need to wait for Maria. She would demonstrate that she was physically recovered at least. Awkwardly, she bundled her hair into a shower cap and adjusted the shower. So far, so good. Feeling rather pleased with herself, she slopped delicately perfumed bath gel over as much of her as she could reach with one hand and stepped under the shower. The cool spray stung her back, washing off the gel and invigorating her. Carefully she kept her left arm stuck out through the shower curtains in order to keep the plaster dry.

Drying herself was not easy, a large bath-sheet does not lend itself to one-handed manipulation, so after an abortive attempt she abandoned the bath-sheet in favour of smaller towels from a neat pile on the shelf by the bath. Now to dress. Panties, bra—no, she could not manage the fastening, so she would have to do without that. A leaf-brown skirt from the wardrobe, a thin, darker brown shirt—awkwardly she fastened the buttons; the cuffs would have to stay loose. She seized a corded velvet waistcoat in a matching brown with satisfaction. That, she reasoned, would conceal her bra-less state.

She laddered two pairs of tights before giving up in disgust. With her head on one side, she decided that her legs were brown and smooth enough to go barelegged, so she pushed her feet into soft sandals and turned her attention to her face. She looked better already, she thought, studying her reflection. Her eyes were clear and bright, her skin had lost the waxy look of yesterday, so she could manage without make-up, but perhaps a little lipstick, that would improve her morale even if it did nothing for her appearance, so she scrabbled through the shallow drawer to find a nice browny-red one and applied it sparingly.

Brushing her hair was easy. Methodically, she counted out a hundred strokes, but doing something with it afterwards was not; however, that was easily overcome. She found a piece of brown ribbon and pushed it into the pocket of her skirt. The first person she saw would be asked to tie it back. Finally, satisfied with her appearance, she made her way downstairs.

The big, gloomy entrance hall was empty and quiet; the *sala*, sunlit and serene, was equally devoid of life. There was no sound from the dining-room and Victoria peeped into its black oak and red velvet magnificence with wide eyes. What a difference daylight made; last night it had looked sombrely wealthy, this morning it was overpowering. She made a mental note to get the enormous gold-tasselled cords that held back the curtains replaced by something a little less awe-inspiring, if she was allowed to do so, and wandered off again down a corridor to stop at a door through which her twitching nose detected the fragrant aroma of coffee.

She entered a reasonably small, bright room and looked about her appreciatively. Sunlight streamed in through wide french windows that seemed to turn one wall into a vast expanse of glass. Through them she could see a lovely little patio with tubs of bright geraniums along the low wall surrounding it and in one corner was some garden furniture, the chairs looking very gay with white paint and colourful plastic-covered seat cushions.

Victoria looked around the room itself with pleasure. The Spanish desire for furniture of hefty proportions, preferably in black oak, hadn't percolated this far, or perhaps it was a more modern addition to the house and furnished more recently. The table and chairs were of a glowing golden pine, as was the sideboard. A tall dresser in the same wood displayed on the shelves, bright pottery plates and saucers in a striking pattern of cream, scarlet and black and matching cups hung from hooks along the edges of the shelves. The walls of the room were the usual plain, unadorned white, but the curtains were of a modern folksy weave in stripes of tobacco and red on a cream ground. A lovely, smiling room. Victoria breathed a sigh of relief. One could have just so much of damask and velvet, not to mention gold cords and tassels!

Rafael looked up from the letter he was reading and rose swiftly to pull out a chair for her. 'Good morning, Victoria. You feel well?'

Victoria produced her piece of ribbon. 'Very well, thank you, and I've managed to shower and dress myself without any help. The result,' she grimaced slightly, 'is far from perfect, as you can see, because I can't use this,' waving her plastered arm. 'I've had to dispense with a couple of items of clothing, but I don't look too bad, do you think? Could you tie my hair back for me, please? I was hungry and I didn't want to wait for Maria.'

'You look quite charming.' He scooped her hair back and tied the ribbon deftly, bending to kiss the nape of her neck. 'You smell delightful also.' He reseated himself and poured her a cup of coffee.

'So I should,' she returned darkly. 'I've used most of what appeared to be a large jar of very expensive bath gel.'

'Maria was to have brought you your breakfast in bed,' he told her firmly.

She waved aside any notion he might have that she should be treated as an invalid. 'Breakfast in bed on a lovely morning like this? Certainly not! I'm not helpless, I've just proved it, haven't I?' Triumphantly she faced him. 'If you'll kindly butter me some toast, I can manage everything else myself and you can go on reading your letters or whatever. I won't disturb you at all.' She took a sip of scalding coffee and relaxed into a silence that lasted until he had finished reading the lengthy letter. During this time, she refilled her coffee cup twice and worked her way steadily through the pile of buttered toast, spooning the marmalade on with a lavish hand.

At last the letter was finished, folded and returned to its envelope, and Rafael raised his head. She poured him another cup of coffee and he stirred it reflectively. 'Have you time to talk, Rafael? There are things I'll have to know.' Her face crinkled in a frown. 'What time does Isabel come down? Do Abuela and Inez breakfast in bed? What do we do all day, because I can't just sit and twiddle my thumbs. What's the relationship between you and Inez . . .?'

'Victoria,' he broke in on her questions, 'your tongue is wagging like a small fussy clock! If you will confine yourself to one question at a time, then I will answer it, but this spate of queries!' He raised his eyebrows eloquently. 'First of all—yes, I do have time to talk for today I have given myself a holiday and also for the rest of the week. No, do not interrupt or I shall have to find a way of silencing your so busy tongue.' He slanted a meaning glance at her mouth which had her blushing fierily. 'Come,' he took her arm and led her to the french windows,' we will sit out on the patio where it is warm and sunny, and in the half hour before Isabel presents herself for breakfast I will endeavour to answer most if not all of your questions.

'Now,' he seated her in one of the quite comfortable cushioned chairs and drawing up another for himself, sat beside her.

Victoria examined him slowly. He looked very well groomed, cream silk shirt open at the neck, coffee-coloured slacks. 'You have very long legs,' she remarked inconsequentially, 'and your eyelashes are preposterous.'

'*Pequeña*,' he might have been speaking to Isabel, 'the length of my legs and the preposterousness of my eyelashes have nothing to do with my household. These two subjects we may discuss later, if you wish, and in more sympathetic surroundings. For the present, I must insist that you keep to the point. And do not smile at me like that or this conversation will degenerate into a much more pleasant though less informative pastime. See, already you are distracting me.' He dropped a light kiss on her mouth. 'And you have marmalade still on your lips. What is wrong with my eyelashes, *por favor*?'

Victoria made her expression serious. 'Now it's you that's wasting time.' She wiped her mouth vigorously with her handkerchief and removed the last trace of a smile from her lips. 'Right! I'm ready, fire away. Start at the beginning, go right through to the end and then stop. That's what the White King said in *Alice*.'

'Red Queens, White Kings! *Mi esposa*, what shall I do with you?' Rafael had begun to sound exasperated. 'We will, for the minute, forget this Alice, hmm? Abuela is my grandmother and Inez is the cousin of Consuelo who was my wife and the mother of Isabel. When

Consuelo died, I brought Abuela here from Granada where she had been living with her maid in a small house which I have there. She was not in good health, the death of Consuelo had shocked her and I considered that she would be better living here than in Granada with only old Sancha for company. She had not so many friends left there, she was outliving most of her contemporaries. I thought also that she would have an added interest in the wellbeing of Isabel, who is her granddaughter.'

'Is she very old?' Victoria wrinkled up her face. 'I'm not very good at judging people's ages.'

'Abuela has eighty-two years,' he smiled at her look of amazement. 'Her mind is still powerful although she becomes increasingly frail. Sancha, her maid, is a little younger, I think about seventy-five. You have not met her yet, you have a treat in store.'

At this rate, Victoria thought, they would still be talking about Abuela at tea time, so she hurried him on a little. 'Inez?'

'Inez,' he shrugged. 'Inez was a cousin of Consuelo, they were brought up together in Madrid and during our brief marriage she spent many weeks here with my wife. After Consuelo's death, Inez suggested that she should come here to help Abuela run this house and to assist with the care of Isabel. It was a satisfactory arrangement for me, my business was expanding and I was frequently away for weeks at a time. I could safely go and leave all the household affairs in Inez's capable hands. She is a good organiser.'

'She's very beautiful.' Victoria sounded wistful.

'Very!' He was emphatic, and she nearly asked 'Why didn't you marry her?' when she hesitated and then decided to abandon the subject of Inez.

'Isabel—her leg, was she born like that?'

Rafael's face darkened and his mouth tinned to a straight line. 'No. There was an accident when she was four years old. She stumbled in the path of a horsedrawn vehicle. By the Grace of God, the horse avoided her, but one wheel of the cart passed over her leg and ankle. She has worn the support ever since.'

'Can't anybody do anything?' Victoria thought of the little girl, so pretty and with the promise of great beauty. Not only that, Isabel was a nice child with a pleasant, happy disposition. It didn't seem fair that she should never walk properly.

'My letter this morning, it was from an orthopaedic surgeon who is coming here to San Sebastian in October—an Englishman. There is fresh hope, not hope of a complete cure, you understand. Isabel will always limp, but enough may be done to the smashed bones so that she no longer needs to wear the brace. This Englishman will examine Isabel when he comes to Spain. Meanwhile,' he raised a finger, 'you will not speak of this, not to Abuela. I do not wish to raise false hopes again.'

Abruptly he changed the subject before Victoria had a chance to ask whether Isabel might be allowed to know.

'As to what you do today, while Isabel breakfasts, you will ready yourself and we will drive down to San Sebastian. We will have lunch at an hotel and afterwards we will mingle with the tourists, dispose ourselves on the beach perhaps, take a ride in a speedboat, look in the shops or do whatever you choose. I have a small business matter to which I must attend, but it will not take long, so you can amuse yourselves or wait for me in my office. Then we will find a restaurant that serves tea—there are several because San Sebastian is quite popular with the English tourists—and afterwards we will make our way home. Does this plan please you, Señora Alvarez?'

'It sounds marvellous,' Victoria sparkled at him, forgetting all about Inez for the moment. 'We'll be home in time for Isabel's supper?' she questioned.

'And for our own meal, so that we shall not break Pilar's heart by not being here to eat her good dinner.'

'Will Inez be coming with us?' It was an apparently idle question, but her fingers tapped nervously on the arm of her chair.

'No.' He shook his head. 'Unfortunately Inez is not a good traveller. For a long journey with a definite reason, she will travel, but it gives her acute discomfort, so she does not, how do you say it? joyride?'

'That's exactly how you say it,' Victoria nodded her red head, then, 'The journey to Lourdes,' she questioned. 'That had a definite reason?'

'But of course!' Rafael looked at her in surprise. 'Inez had planned it all last year, thinking that there was a slight possibility that it would help Isabel. There have been some quite remarkable cures,' he added thoughtfully, but even as he said it she heard the angry note creeping back into his voice and watched his face harden.

'Though why you all had to go there when both Carlos and myself were away I do not know—and as for your foolhardiness in attempting to return at night, alone and without proper rest. . . .' There was a glitter of something like rage in his eyes. 'Each time I think of it, I become more angry. Little idiot, you could have been killed!'

'I'm sorry,' she looked bewildered, 'but I can't explain, you know I can't. It wouldn't be so bad if I knew what you were talking about, but I don't.'

'I am talking about five days when it seemed that you had vanished from the face of the earth. There was no news of you.' He had risen from his chair and reached out to grasp her shoulders, his fingers biting painfully into her flesh. 'Dios!' He ground the word out between his teeth and shook her none too gently. 'I nearly went mad, do you know that? Inez was convinced that you had run away, perhaps to England, but I could not think so. You would not have gone without telling me first and you would not have taken my car.'

'Why should I want to run away?' She looked at him with a worried frown. 'Weren't we happy? Had we been quarrelling?'

'We were perfectly happy!' His smile was very faint. 'As to whether we had been quarrelling, we did that so often that it was no longer of importance. You lost your temper on average about once every forty-eight hours.'

'I thought you said that we were happy? How could we have been happy, living like that?' Her eyes were wide with disbelief. 'It must have been a horrid existence. No wonder I ran away from you!'

'But you did not! When you were found, you were on your way back to me.'

Victoria was silenced and mulled this fact over in her brain. 'Perhaps I was just coming to return your car,' she suggested after some thought.

'*Estupida!*' He shook her again.

'That's the second time you've suggested that I'm an idiot,' she flared, her eyes sliding sideways to see if there was anything near at hand which she could use as a weapon. 'I know I'm not beautiful or graceful or any of the other things you ought to have in a wife, but I'm not an idiot—unless marrying you makes me one.'

'I think I have proved my point,' Rafael was smiling. 'We are quarrelling, but is it enough to make you wish to leave me?'

'You mean that you deliberately made me lose my temper!' Rage choked her and her eyes glowed green in their hazel depths.

'Mmm.' He pulled her to her feet. 'But you, *querida*, you also make me lose mine. When I arrived at that hospital and saw you, white and frightened, I very much wished to chastise you for frightening me so. The only thing that stopped me, I think, was the realisation that you didn't know me. You sat there with those childish plaits of hair and big, frightened, unknowing eyes, and you looked very little older than Isabel and far less able to take care of yourself. You will never do a thing like that to me again, you understand?' He pulled her close. 'I was to have left you in that place for another week, the doctors wished it, but I could not. I must have you here, under my eyes, so that I may be sure you do not do these mad things again.' The savage note had died out of his voice. 'You did not mind this, Victoria? It was important to me.'

She shook her head, wiping tears from her eyes with the back of her hand. She searched for a handkerchief, but could only find the one she had used at breakfast, a stupid thing, a silly lace-edged scrap of lawn, not nearly big enough. She sniffed despairingly. Rafael proffered a large white one which she accepted gratefully, mopping up her futile tears; then she blew her nose in it, screwed it up into a big damp ball and stuffed it in her pocket.

He pushed her away from him, still holding her, and looked down at her face. 'You will not do such a thing again,' he insisted. 'You will promise me that.' His arms drew her close and his mouth strayed over her bright hair. Gently he tugged at it, tilting her face upwards.

'Promise?' he demanded.

'Promise,' she answered blissfully as Isabel called from the breakfast room.

The drive down to San Sebastian took them in a wide sweep past Pamplona. Victoria found it quite uncanny to come down from the fresh greenness of the country-side about the Casa on to the yellow and brown plain where Pamplona stood sleepily in the hot air and the blinding sunshine. It would be stifling in the city by noon, Rafael remarked.

'Is it always so quiet here?' Victoria looked at shuttered windows and hot yellow walls. Her husband shook his head.

'Only for fifty-one weeks in the year,' he murmured.

'What happens on the fifty-second?' she demanded.

'The fifty-second week is San Fermin—a festival when they run the bulls through the town and young men try to outrun them. Pamplona is not popular with tourists until that week, then it is crowded. After the end of the festivities, Pamplona goes back to sleep again until the next San Fermin. I brought you here to the last San Fermin in July, and you were rather frightened.'

'Does anyone get hurt?' She had gone rather pale as she thought of wild bulls rampaging through the streets.

'The usual number of hotheads get maimed or killed,' he answered callously. There are a great number of photographers here for the festival and it is a great honour to be photographed, especially if one is in a very dangerous position, about to be tossed or gored. The pictures are displayed with pride in all the restaurants.'

Outside Pamplona they took the wide new road to San Sebastian, but it was only a short stretch, for after a few miles the road started climbing over the hills between Pamplona and the coast. Life was a little more primitive here. Victoria recalled the streams of traffic which they had left not long ago and compared them with the patient yoked oxen which were drawing a cart along just in front of the car.

They ran down into San Sebastian just after noon. It was hot, but there was a cool breeze from the sea. The city looked very fresh and clean along the sea front, almost new-looking for such an old place, with wide streets and beautiful, imposing buildings in the centre.

Isabel gave her a small history lesson, leaning over the front seats of the car, her curls bobbing between them. San Sebastian had been all but destroyed at the end of the Peninsular War, Victoria learned, and the town council had rebuilt it afterwards on modern lines with wide streets and avenues and imposing buildings.

Rafael nodded and added that his daughter had the usual facility of remembering only part of her history. Such mundane things as dates and names were, in the opinion of Isabel, hardly worth bothering about!

They were to have gone to an hotel, but in a side street behind the esplanade, Isabel and Victoria found a seafood restaurant where the displayed dishes had been so beautifully and temptingly arranged that Rafael grimaced and said he would have no peace until he took them inside.

It didn't look his sort of place and Victoria thought that he probably considered that he was slumming, but for all that she gave him full marks for slumming beautifully. They ate prawns and *langostinos*, like tiny lobsters, fluffy tortillas filled with mushrooms and cheese, and washed the whole lot down with glasses of Sangria.

After lunch they sat on chairs by the sea front. Isabel chattered happily of this and that while Victoria dozed, rousing now and then as one after another bikini-clad beauty arrived, oiled herself and arranged herself on a carefully spread towel or beach mat to toast to a deep mahogany. Some of the bikinis were so brief that she blinked unbelievingly.

'I thought that Spanish girls didn't. . . .' she began.

'These are probably French.' Rafael eyed a slender blonde in the minimum of yellow with a gleam in his eye. 'San Sebastian is very close to the border and it is one of the few places where you find French holiday-makers. They usually stay in France, but here the prices are lower and it is only a short journey, so the French come.'

'You sound as if you didn't like them much. Do you?'

'Individually, yes. Collectively, no.' Rafael was quite definite.

'But . . .' she stammered, 'I thought that all Europeans. . . .'

'You say Europeans as if we were all alike,' he was curt. 'We're not. We are French or German, Spanish or Italian, Belgian or Dutch. Each nation has its own ways, we have ours. We Spanish are thought to be more backward, but this is not so. We merely have a different set of values.'

He left them in a large emporium in the centre of the city, a store dedicated to the whims and fancies of a large number of tourists. Before he left them, he pressed a large roll of notes into Victoria's hot and, by this time, sticky hand; she and Isabel had been eating ice cream to prevent them feeling hungry before teatime. The overall plan was that Rafael should go and attend to his business while his females amused themselves for half an hour or so, browsing around amid the displayed goods. Then they would all meet in the top floor restaurant of the store, where in pleasant surroundings, if possible at a table near a window overlooking the sea, they would have tea.

Victoria thought that his attitude was stupid in the extreme. To leave two penniless young ladies to browse in a large and luxurious department store was a harmless act, but to provide those two young ladies with fistsful of money was an act of folly and deserved no better than it got! She wondered vaguely why she always felt this mild belligerence towards him in his absence. He was kind, courteous and considerate to everybody, and to herself he was much more than that. A soft colour flamed in her face. Then why did she have a peculiar desire to annoy him, to make him angry?

She took a breath and stared at the money in her hand. He'd asked for trouble, hadn't he? and casting discretion to the winds, she and Isabel retreated behind a display of beachwear to assess the amount of his generosity and to decide how best it was to be spent or wasted depending on how one looked at it. After all, she consoled herself, a man who could dismiss the loss of

a large and valuable car without turning a hair, even
say it was of no consequence, and who would, to get his
own way, cheerfully fund a new hospital ward for children, would surely not blink if his wife and daughter
spent a few thousand pesetas to pass an idle half
hour.

Isabel considered the amount to be insufficient for
serious shopping, so it was agreed that it should be
treated as fun money and used accordingly. A miniature
musical box, shaped like a grand piano, took Isabel's
fancy. It tinkled out *Valencia* when the lid was lifted.
This was purchased and neatly wrapped to be disposed
tenderly in a plastic carrier bag specially purchased for
the purpose.

In the evening wear department, Victoria's eye was
caught by a very beautiful evening gown. In thin white
silk, it fell straight, rather like an ancient Greek chiton,
being caught at the waist by a simple gold cord with
fringed ends. A glance at the ticket convinced her that it
would fit perfectly, a further glance also convinced her
that they had insufficient money to purchase it.
Regretfully, she and Isabel, who had shown her re-
markably good taste by admiring the dress at length,
turned away and headed for Children's Wear. Here they
found, alongside the playsuits and beachwear, racks of
jeans and tee-shirts in various colours. Isabel's face grew
wistful.

'I have always wanted to wear such clothes during
the school holidays,' she confided in a whisper. 'But
Tía Inez does not approve of such things.' She tweaked
the frilled skirt of her broderie anglaise dress. 'None of
the children we have seen today are wearing clothes like
this!'

The mention of Inez was like a red rag to Victoria's
bull. Firmly, she called up a saleslady and despatched her
and Isabel into a curtained fitting-room with armsful of
jeans and tee-shirts while she sat herself down on a

nearby chair to await the parade. It was so that Rafael found her, just as his daughter emerged from the fitting room, her nether regions clad in navy blue jeans, the bottoms of which were turned up in cuffs in the regulation manner; and her upper parts decently clothed in a white tee-shirt which announced to the world, in big black letters, that its wearer was a graduate of the California State Prison of Alcatraz.

Isabel limped forward, her eyes shining. It was a great improvement, thought Victoria. The jeans covered the brace so that Isabel's limp seemed much less noticeable. Victoria found herself looking up at her husband with eloquent eyes. She was almost praying that he would smile approvingly. He did better.

'Most becoming, *hija*,' he chuckled. 'You have, or intend to have, more of these garments, I hope? One pair of jeans and one shirt can become soiled very quickly.'

Isabel riffled gleefully through the racks, her small fingers deftly selecting and rejecting until the pile of garments in the saleslady's arms began to assume gigantic proportions. Victoria, with a thwarted expression, proffered the remaining notes in her hand. She had intended that they should have all been spent by the Rafael arrived, but she hadn't been quick enough, and her eyes glowed with a fine rage.

'And I see that my wife is not a spendthrift. Is there nothing you require, *amada*?'

She shook her head briefly. 'Not unless you count some jigsaw puzzles and poster paints and, of course, some paper. Playthings for Isabel,' she explained. 'But I don't think we'll get them here—another shop, perhaps.'

'There is the dress, Victoria, don't forget about that. It's a beautiful dress,' Isabel turned to her father. 'There wasn't enough money to buy it, but it's so lovely and Victoria liked it.'

'I didn't want it that badly,' she said in a gruff little voice. 'I couldn't wear it yet anyway, and apart from the fact that I already have a cupboard full, it's very expensive.'

'We shall see this dress.' Rafael took Isabel's hand. 'You shall show me.'

Isabel jigged while her own parcel was wrapped and waited with ill-concealed impatience for the payment to be made before she was off to the Ladies' Wear department.

Rafael stood before the dress and looked from it to his wife and back again. 'It will fit?' Hot-faced, Victoria nodded and the sale was completed in soft Spanish. A girl removed it tenderly from the model on which it had been draped and after folding it in layers of tissue, placed it in a separate box within a carrier.

'I shall expect you to wear that. The first evening you are without your plaster should be a good time. We will make it an occasion.' He smiled down at her.

Victoria spent the hour before getting dressed for dinner in a kind of informal family room at the very back of the house. Here there were comfortable chairs in loose coverings of chocolate brown linen, a stereo record player stood against one wall, there were a few low tables and acres of floor space. Victoria was on the floor with two trays in front of her. One tray contained the bare outline of a large and complicated jigsaw puzzle and the other tray held the five hundred or so other pieces which she had not placed yet. As Rafael came in, she rose from her knees.

'It's very difficult, Isabel's much better at it than I am,' she said as she scrambled to her feet. She looked at the outline and then again at the tray full of jumbled pieces. 'It's rather like me,' she said morbidly. 'There's just an outline of me. There's nothing in the middle. It makes one very unsure of oneself,' she added forlornly.

This plaintive speech caused her husband to frown.

'It is nothing of the sort.' He was practical. 'You are probably hungry, which is what is making you feel that there is nothing in the middle. I suggest that you go and dress for dinner.'

'Insensitive creature!' Victoria snorted.

'Not insensitive at all,' he denied. 'You are behaving like a foolish child, so you will be treated like one.'

Dispiritedly, she climbed the stairs. He was an insensitive brute and she wished that she had frittered away every peseta of his money. She was glad that she had—or rather he had—bought that expensive dress. She wished it had cost twice as much. She wished that she had never married him. At this point, her mind did a little flop. Why had she married him? It was something to mull over, something that didn't make sense.

Maria was waiting for her in the bedroom, full of explanations of the re-allocation of her duties. Her cousin Raquel had come up from the village, but she, Maria, wished to continue to attend the Señora while an attendant was required. Raquel would therefore help in the kitchen and about the house, leaving the more delicate work, such as the bathing and dressing of the Señora to herself. She hoped that the Señora would find this arrangement agreeable.

The Señora smiled with spurious warmth as she levered herself into the bath. She surveyed her plastered arm with a deal of disfavour. Another four weeks had to pass before the plaster was removed and already she was heartily sick of it. Moreover, it was beginning to look distinctly grubby. There was another caftan spread on the bed waiting for her to put it on. A black silk one with gold embroidery. She eyed it with disfavour. The bath had done nothing to restore her spirits.

Nevertheless, within twenty minutes of going upstairs, Victoria was sat on Isabel's bed reading an Enid Blyton story aloud, and when that was finished, listening to Isabel's chatter about the shops in San Sebastian which, according to the little girl, were so much bigger and better than those in Pamplona. After that, they chose another tee-shirt for Isabel to wear the next morning, one that had DEATH ROW—SING-SING blazoned across the chest.

'You are tired, I think,' Rafael told her as they went down the stairs. 'So tonight you will eat your dinner, but there will be no sitting in the *sala* afterwards. You will go back to our room when you have eaten and Maria will put you to bed. I have about an hour's work to do and then I shall join you.'

For the last half hour Victoria had been wishing that she could do that very thing, but as soon as she heard him say it aloud, it was the last thing she wanted. He had not suggested it, he had told her! He was laying down the law! Her back snapped straight and she pooh-poohed his decree.

'I'm looking forward to my dinner and a pleasant chat with Abuela afterwards. I'm not going to be treated as an invalid, sent off to bed with a glass of hot milk. I shall stay up as long as I like!' Green glints in her hazel eyes dared him to contradict her.

He merely smiled down at her. 'As you wish, *querida*. But knowing your dislike of them, I merely thought you would wish to be in bed and asleep before the storm breaks.'

'We're going to have a storm?'

'Certainly. Had you not realised? Since about four o'clock the air has been growing heavy, even Abuela has complained of a headache. It will be a big one, I think.' He glanced down at his wrist watch. 'Carlos has already attended to the generator, a task he usually leaves until after dinner.' He caught her arm in a firm hold, pulling her round to face him. 'You will do as I say. Hmm? Abuela, you will find, will also retire early and Inez went this afternoon to stay with friends in Pamplona for a week or so, Abuela tells me. Tomorrow we will have a lazy day here and you will *not* present yourself for an early breakfast.'

The storm which Rafael had predicted broke before midnight. Victoria woke to the splitting crash of thunder and the vicious spears of blue-white lightning which illuminated the bedroom. It rolled and smashed around the mountains for more than an hour, while the air grew steadily hotter and became more still. From the beginning she lay rigid under a single sheet and felt herself become bathed in perspiration. An enormous wind blew up and torrential rain followed after a while, but the thunder continued to rumble and mutter threateningly for over an hour afterwards.

When the storm was at its height, she lay trembling, whimpering softly when overhead, thunder and lightning erupted together in a savage scream and a light so bright that it penetrated her closely shut eyelids, illuminated everything in the room. Just as she thought she could stand no more, that she would start screaming with terror. Rafael's arm drew her close and she buried her head against his chest. Thick, springy hair tickled her nose and the gold medallion he wore pressed against her cheek, hard and smooth. Convulsively she grasped him, burrowing against him like some small, frightened animal. She found her head pushed up and away and then tilted towards him as his mouth in the darkness found hers, sweet, warm and demanding. Close to her ear she heard his voice, soft and thickened, whispering in Spanish, words she did not understand but which made her shivering terror die away, to be replaced by a warm glow, a rising need. The storm outside ceased to have much importance; all that mattered was to get closer to him. Her hand clenched on the thick hair at the back of his head and she moaned softly as her pyjama jacket was unbuttoned and importunate hands found her breasts. His mouth slid down her neck, coaxing, caressing, to tease the sensitive hollow at its base. Of its own volition, her body moved seductively against him, she heard the swift intake of his breath, felt the weight of him, the hard demand, and was filled by a need as great as his, and later, much later, with a warm, lazy, exhausted contentment.

She woke late to a clean fresh day and a sparkling blue sky. Lazily she lay and watched small white clouds chase each other across the sky. The bedroom door opened to admit Maria with a tray, closely followed by Rafael. From under her lashes she studied him. He looked his usual well-groomed self, imperturbable, black hair smooth and unruffled, a thin black shirt open at the neck, impeccably creased black trousers. A faint scent of aftershave caught at Victoria's nostrils while his grey eyes in their ridiculously feminine fringe of dark lashes gleamed down at her. She was suddenly conscious of her bare shoulders and tumbled hair and she slid down in the bed, pulling the sheet up to her chin. He studied her keenly for a few moments.

'You look much better this morning, *querida*.' He turned away to pour coffee into cups. 'More rested, more relaxed.' His words fell on empty space, for as soon as his back was turned, Victoria had slid swiftly out of bed, flung a robe about herself and fled to the bathroom.

Once there, she dashed under the shower, emerging gasping with the shock of the cold water. She towelled herself briefly and struggled her still damp body into her old green velvet robe of which she was so fond. She dragged a brush through her hair, wincing as she encountered several tangles. Finally satisfied that she no longer looked like a slut, she rejoined him and accepted the cup of coffee gratefully.

'You slept well, I trust?' His eyes glanced down wickedly at her.

'I slept very well, thank you,' she answered him sedately. 'The storm—did it do much damage?'

'Not here. Further up the French coast, it was violent. The radio says that it cut great swathes through the pine forests north of Bayonne.' He looked hard at her. 'You will remain in bed until lunchtime.' Once again it was an order, softly spoken and with a smile to accompany it, but still an order. Victoria opened her mouth to protest, but before she could utter a word his hand closed her lips. 'No, there is nothing for you to do. Isabel is happily engaged with her new jigsaw puzzle, and if she requires assistance no doubt Abuela will provide it. Go back to bed, *señora*, and don't look so mutinous. Tonight we dine with the Martinez family who live some ten miles from here, so it will be late when we return.' He bent over and kissed her parted lips. She felt the leap in her blood and wondered if he felt it too, but the dark face gave nothing away.

The Martinez family were charming. They were a happy contented pair. Señor Martinez seemed to be at least twenty years older than his plump, busy-looking wife, who Victoria decided was in her early forties. Señora Martinez was wrapped up in her home and her family and Señor Martinez was equally wrapped up in the wine which his family produced and which he exported. Juan, the son, was an intense youth with a fine disregard for the opinions of anyone outside his own age group and a fine pair of languishing black eyes. Olivia, his sister, was demure to the point of silence. She had but lately finished her education at a convent boarding school and was obviously finding the transition to adult life a little difficult. Even so, dinner was a gay meal, probably due to the two glasses of sherry which Señor Martinez insisted should be drunk before they sat down to dinner.

Señora Martinez was proud of their home, it was evident in the gleam of polish which reflected light from every polishable surface.

'This is the house of our dreams,' she told Victoria.

'All my married life has been spent in the house at Jerez, so cold, so inconvenient, so big.' She waved expressive, heavily beringed hands. 'We promised ourselves that when Lorenzo retired from the business, we would build ourselves a house which would be as we wanted it—far from the vineyards, here in the cooler green of Navarre. Not that Lorenzo has retired properly,' Señora Martinez gave a rich laugh. 'Still he sees to the shipping of the wine and the family is appreciative of his abilities, but we can live here as we wish. I am not surrounded by vines, hectare upon hectare of them, nor need we worry about the mould on the leaves or the little black flies which can ruin the harvest.' Señora Martinez sighed with evident contentment.

Juan's eyes, after two glasses of sherry, several more of table wine and a large helping of brandy with his coffee, languished all over Victoria. She found him gazing at her with a sad soulful look that would have set the heartbeats of a teenage girl thundering. Sensibly, she put it down to an excessive consumption of alcohol together with a lack of the right type of female company. She turned her attention back to his father, who was, in her opinion, far better company and a more stimulating companion. Determinedly she ignored the spaniel-like appeal in the young man's eyes. It made her feel hot, uncomfortable and faintly nauseated.

It was past midnight when she and Rafael arrived home. They let themselves into the silent house and crept quietly up the stairs. Abuela was a notoriously light sleeper and once the old lady awakened she found it difficult to go back to sleep. So it was not until they were in their bedroom and Victoria had discarded her coat that Rafael took her shoulders and turned her towards him.

'The devotion of the young Juan, it did not disturb you?'

Victoria gazed at him wonderingly. 'Certainly not! He

is, as you said, very young. He'll forget all about it as soon as he gets among others of his own age. Did it disturb you?'

'No, *querida*, not at all.' He sounded amused. 'As you say, he will forget very soon, but until he does, you will probably find him—er—hanging around. We live not so far from his home and he is the proud possessor of a brand new sports car.'

'He'll get no encouragement from me,' she flared.

'I know that also. Even I, who am your husband, get little encouragement from you.'

'I didn't know,' she answered pertly, 'that husbands need encouragement.'

'Sometimes,' he whispered, nuzzling a sensitive spot behind and just below her ear.

She rumpled his hair as she felt his teeth biting the lobe of her ear.

'Well, you certainly don't!' she gasped.

CHAPTER FIVE

VICTORIA sat on the patio outside the breakfast room, a glass and a tall jug of lemonade on the table beside her. Idly she watched the garden. Tomás, the young man who ran the sizeable farm attached to the Casa, was coming up the path. Soon he would turn to go around to the kitchen door, but before he did, Maria would come to meet him. Yes, here she came, a flying figure in black, her white apron whipping in the breeze.

The two young things would talk for a while, then Maria would take the basket containing the eggs and butter into the house. It was a daily ritual. Pilar knew all about it, of course, she kept a very close eye on her elder daughter, but Tomás and Maria loved their, as they thought, stolen meetings. One day, Victoria supposed, when Pilar judged that little Carlota was old enough to take Maria's place, Maria and Tomás would marry and Maria would move down to the whitewashed farmhouse with its outside staircase which held a tub of geraniums on each step so that from a distance it looked like a diagonal line of colour against the wall.

A wave of near-envy swept over Victoria and with a slightly unsteady hand she poured herself a glassful of lemonade, feeling again the depression which had weighed her down ever since Rafael had gone off on a business trip.

She was not discontented, she told herself. Not a bit! As a husband, Rafael was very satisfactory, very satisfactory indeed. Of course, he never mentioned love or anything like that, but it was a good marriage. She told herself the same thing at least twice a day, every day. He was kind and considerate, passionate and very generous. He was also infuriating, enigmatic and intensely appreciative of good-looking women.

She breathed a sigh of relief when he went away, telling herself that now, on her own and without his seducing hands and mouth, she would be her own woman. Yes, it was with definite relief that she waved him goodbye and then went hastily to the calendar to mark off the days, hours and minutes of his absence—she wouldn't even think of him while he was away—and promptly found herself thinking of little else. She wouldn't speak of him or mention his name. She kept this iron resolve, but listened avidly to every word Abuela and the others said about him. And they were many.

She threw herself into the task of preparing rooms for Abuela and Sancha on the ground floor so that Abuela should be spared the climb up the stairs. There were three little-used rooms at the far end of the rambling extension. One of them, a pleasant, sunny little sitting-room, would remain just that. Two others leading from it were to be converted into bedrooms and another room, just across the corridor, would be turned into a bathroom. Carlos arranged the plumber for her and she watched the creation of the bathroom with delight. She and Abuela pored over catalogues of bathroom suites, chose materials for curtains and bedspreads and decided what furniture could be moved down from upstairs. Sancha viewed the move with deep suspicion.

'Pay no attention,' Abuela advised tartly. 'Sancha is, as I am, old. When one is old one dislikes change. It means noise and inconvenience and worst of all getting used to new surroundings when it seems that there is so little time left. . . .'

'What utter nonsense!' Victoria injected a bracing note into her voice. 'Now what about these curtains? It was the rose-coloured velvet for your room, wasn't it, and Sancha is to have green. Have I got that right?'

Now all the preparations were complete and the rooms ready for occupation. The new bathroom suite had been duly admired—bath, handbasin, toilet and bidet all in avocado green with creamy tiles to set it off. In the bedrooms, neat built-in wardrobes filled the alcoves and fresh paint and curtains made them look very attractive. All that remained to be done was the transfer of clothing and personal posessions, but was Victoria allowed to take a hand in this final act? No, she was not!

Maria, Carlota and Raquel, under the direction of Carlos, would attend to this final stage. If other assistance was required, Pilar was ready and waiting. 'The Señora, said Carlos, his pleasant, wrinkled face full of concern, was not to exhaust herself. She must not soil her hands with such tasks! The Señora should sit on the patio where the air was fresh and cool. She should observe the Doña Luisa who sat quietly in the *sala* with the little one. All should be as the Señora desired.' In other words, the Señora thought waspishly, 'Don't interfere!'

It took several seconds to remember that when Carlos spoke of the Doña Luisa, he meant Abuela, and during those seconds Carlos had vanished upstairs. So Victoria had taken herself off peevishly to the patio. Abuela joined her there just before lunch.

Old Sancha had apparently taken upon herself the direction of the transport of such items as she deemed indispensable to her mode of life, one of which was a case of small stuffed birds. It was a large case and it had been dropped with, to Sancha, serious consequences. Fortunately, neither glass nor birds had suffered serious damage, but one small bird had fallen from its perch and now lay on its back on the floor of the case. Abuela chuckled delightedly.

'So natural now, niña. Many small birds perched and supposedly singing over one dead bird. Sancha is, of course, deeply upset. She sits now in what was our sitting room, guarding her treasures in case some other ill befalls them.' An expression of concern passed fleetingly over the old ivory of her face. 'Could you not go, *niña*, and perhaps coax her to come down and sit with me? She will upset the others and there will be little work done.'

Victoria found the old maid seated bolt upright in the one remaining chair. Her thin hair was drawn back severely into a tight grey bun and her brown, wrinkled face was set in lines of grim resolve while her small black eyes glittered balefully behind a pair of steel-rimmed spectacles. On the table beside her were her treasures. An old Venetian goblet in ruby red glass, the last one of a set, Victoria supposed. There were two or three porcelain figurines, each one broken at some time and carefully mended, a large and noisy alarm clock with a loud, brazen tick, a large needlework basket and several plastic bags containing knitting wool, needles and partly finished garments.

Victoria choked back her amusement while Sancha glared defiantly through the steel-rimmed spectacles. Each article, Victoria noticed, with the exception of the alarm clock and the plastic bags, must have originally belonged to Abuela. Sancha's slippers were a discarded pair of her mistress's, as was the cardigan draped around the old maid's shoulders. Victoria's face softened. It was obvious that Sancha considered any of the Abuela's cast-offs to be her perquisite whether or not they suited or fitted her. The cardigan was much too big and the lavender shade of wool did not become Sancha's walnut-coloured complexion.

'Come down to lunch, Sancha,' she pleaded. 'Doña Luisa has need of you. She is sitting on the patio and I think she may be getting chilled. Perhaps if you brought a shawl, you could persuade her to come indoors.'

As she half expected, the appeal made no impression. Sancha continued to sit, rather like a small dog told to

'Guard' and which would not be moved.

'Do come,' Victoria wheedled. 'You know how determined Doña Luisa is. If you don't come, she will still be sitting there at dinnertime.'

'Doña Luisa is wearing only thin slippers.' Sancha exploded into action, lifting the lid of an old chest and burying her head in it. 'A moment while I find a wrap. I shall also bring shoes, and if, while I am away, any of these idle, good-for-nothing servants to whom Don Rafael pays so much money breaks anything else or does any damage to the possessions of my mistress, I will chastise them myself. Already, *señora*,' she wailed, 'they have dropped my beautiful birds, who will never be the same again. Modern servants—ay-ay!' Her head and shoulders by this time deep in the chest, her voice emerged somewhat muffled as she fulminated upon the slapdash ways of Pilar who had the muscles of an ox and the daintiness of that same animal, of Maria, who thought only of meeting Tomás in secluded parts of the garden when she should be busy with her vacuum cleaner. Vacuum cleaners! Sancha snorted and went on to describe the proper way of cleaning, a way which would reduce the soft Maria to a physical wreck, thereby making it impossible for her to chase Tomás round the garden hedges at least three times a day!

Victoria pointed out that such physical labour on Maria's part might also make her incapable of running fast enough when Tomás chased her, and then, Victoria questioned, what would happen?

Sancha emerged from the chest, woolly shawls clasped to her flat bosom and tut-tutted, although there was a definite softening of her wrinkled little face.

'Then, *señora*, we should have a wedding, a proper wedding such as we were denied when you and Don Rafael were so quietly married. A wedding and a fiesta. There would be many people coming, for Pilar is of a large family and there would be music, dancing, drinking and gaiety until very late, perhaps until dawn, and afterwards we should see if Maria had so much idle time in which to chase Tomás around, how do you say it, the gooseberry bushes?'

After lunch, Victoria went prospecting outside. The garden, she discovered, was of a considerable size, and after examining it she wandered around to the back of the house, to what had once been the coach house and stables. In the dimness of the stables she could hear soft movements with now and then a gentle stamp and a soft whicker. Closer inspection revealed a large black horse who eyed her contemptuously down his Roman nose. There was a light graceful mare and in the end stall, a bright-eyed pony—Isabel's, she guessed. Horses were not Victoria's favourite animal, so after scratching the pony's head, she emerged once more into the sunlight.

The next building was the coach house, converted now to a garage. The door was partly ajar, so she entered. The big black Mercedes stood there in all its sleek splendour, on the other side stood a large and antiquated Rolls-Royce, practically a vintage piece, its huge headlamps and squared-off bonnet gleaming with the labour of loving hands. Neatly sandwiched between these two aristocrats of the road stood an impertinent little Citroën 2CV in a violent shade of green. There was room there for another car, probably the one Rafael was using on his trip.

Victoria's eyes were drawn back to the Citroën. It did not seem at all overawed by its stable companions, in fact it had a gay insouciance about it, a raffish air. She felt rather sympathetic towards it and moved closer, amused at the contrast between dignity and downright impertinence.

It was then that she noticed the British number plates. At first they didn't register in her mind, then after glancing at the ridiculous side windows which opened like a greenhouse ventilator, she took in the right hand-drive. Victoria knew as she walked to the back what she would find, and it was there: 'EMILY' in big flowing letters, painted in black against the bright green of the boot lid. This was her car! Not that she remembered it at all, but she had an inward conviction.

The door opened easily under her hand and she slid behind the wheel, glancing at the very utilitarian interior. Faintly, inside her head, she heard an amused English voice, a feminine voice, say, 'It does everything that other cars do, but with a difference—and *Vive la Différence*!' But whose voice? She wrinkled her brow, puzzling over it. Her own voice, perhaps? She didn't know the answer.

There were no keys in the ignition and she felt a momentary spasm of annoyance. Who had taken them? Why hadn't anybody, Rafael, Carlos, anybody come bouncing up, the moment she came from the hospital saying, 'Your car is in the garage'? Or even if they'd waited a few days before telling her. She had been here nearly a fortnight and it had never been mentioned. Rafael! she decided, temper spurting. He must have told everybody not to mention it, he must have! He didn't want her mobile. He wanted her stuck in the house, dependent on him or Carlos for transport.

It was just like a man! she hissed between her teeth with outrage. One little accident and she was never to drive again, not even her own car! A typical husband, she raged inwardly. She could drive this little thing with a plaster on her arm, she could drive it if she was encased in plaster from her neck to her hips, and she would!

She marched through the kitchen door, eyes sparkling with determination and red hair flaming in the bright sunlight. Pilar was dozing in a big chair by the window and Carlos was seated at the table, reading a newspaper.

'I would like the keys to my car, please,' Victoria

demanded politely. It wasn't Carlos's fault, he only did as he was told. She would, she decided, be far from polite when Rafael returned.

Carlos's face furrowed. 'The Señor, he has not given me such orders, *señora*.' He sounded worried, and her hard-held temper snapped.

The Señor is not here, Carlos, is he? It is my car, is it not? You may give me the keys now. When the Señor returns, I will tell him.'

'The Señora intends to drive the small car?' Carlos still looked worried, but he must have had a sudden flash of inspiration, for his face cleared and he smiled.

'The Señora will permit that I accompany her so that I may be assured of her safety? The Señora's arm might prove troublesome.'

The Señora, her temper gone suddenly off the boil, indicated her pleasure at this suggestion. Pilar, woken by voices, was preparing fresh coffee and sputtered at her husband in soft Spanish.

Victoria and Carlos left half an hour later, bearing with them a flask of coffee and some small cakes. The canvas roof of the 2CV had been rolled back and secured, Carlos had minutely inspected the engine oil and rubbed away some fingermarks that were disfiguring the bonnet. The lights had been tested; side, head and flashers, as had the indicators. The tyre pressures had been taken, including the spare wheel, and a can of petrol had been put in the boot.

Such precautions were necessary in Navarre, Carlos informed her. In this country, one could travel many miles without seeing even a petrol pump, much less a garage, and should such a thing as a puncture occur, how would the Señora have managed? She could not have changed a wheel. Victoria admitted the justice of these remarks, even to herself, and smiled warmly at Carlos as she piloted the little car through the gates.

'If we go this way,' Carlos pointed, 'we go on the

road to Candanchu. There is a ruined church at Canfranc and beautiful streams wherein are many fish. There will be flowers and places where one may park the car and walk among old hedges which smell of lemon.' Obediently, Victoria turned the wheel and the little Citroën roared off up the road. The wind, as they penetrated farther into the mountains, was quite chilly, although the sun shone brightly. They stopped at Canfranc for a refreshing cup of coffee and to munch a cake or so, Carlos taking his refreshment to what he considered to be a proper distance while his mistress consumed hers inside the car.

She found that she was quite glad that Carlos had come with her; her arm had started to ache when she was no more than five miles from the Casa and now the ache had developed into a nagging throb. Perhaps she would not rail at Rafael when he returned. She would simply say, and sweetly, of course, that she had tried out the little car for something to do. She would certainly ask Carlos to drive back. Rafael couldn't possibly argue with her behaviour. She had done just as she should.

'Maybe tomorrow, if you aren't busy, we could go out again, take Señorita Isabel with us and have the whole afternoon,' she suggested.

Carlos nodded, not taking his eyes from the road. He would be most happy to accompany the Señora and the Señorita Isabel. Pilar would be warned and would have everything ready. The little car, he added, was a good vehicle, it had, he searched around for an English word, it had courage. The Citroën snorted its way along gently as if pleased with this compliment, passing a rear-engined Seat with a nasal toot of its very French horn.

The week passed quickly after that. Mornings were spent with Abuela or Isabel since Inez had extended her stay in Pamplona. She had even sent a horse box to convey the stallion and the mare down there for a few

days. Isabel petted her pony, leading him out to a small
paddock each morning so that he could browse the fresh
green grass and trot about, shying at fluttering leaves or
small birds, pretending to be frightened. He grew accus-
tomed to waiting for them each day and snorted blissfully when they came, his head over the lower portion
of the door and his bright intelligent eyes watching their
every movement.

After lunch each day, Victoria and Isabel together
with Carlos jaunted about the countryside, even one day
going as far as the top of Candanchu, but it was too
cold and windy to picnic at such a height, so they
returned to lower ground and ate their cakes and drank
their coffee beside a small river where little fish darted,
glinting silver in the sunlight.

Dinner was brought forward half an hour each evening so that Isabel could join them—'properly dressed',
stipulated Abuela who, while paying lip service to jeans
and tee-shirts, secretly abhorred them. So Isabel presented herself each evening wearing one of her expensive,
exquisite dresses and drank well watered wine with food
which, said Abuela, though it might keep herself awake
half the night with indigestion, would in no way harm
.he child.

It came as quite a surprise to Victoria to find that it
was already Friday and to realise that Rafael would be
home the next day. She was gleeful, time had flown,
and when Abuela asked after her boredom, Victoria was
honest and admitted that she had not felt any. Time
had gone so swiftly that she was almost unaware of the
passing days. But when Isabel went back to the convent
boarding school, as she would at the beginning of
October, Victoria thought she might find time hanging
more heavily on her hands.

Inez returned from Pamplona on that Friday. The
horse box arrived first, closely followed by Inez herself
in Juan Martinez's new sports car, the rear seat piled

high with luggage. Inez presented a smooth, cool cheek to Abuela and then to Victoria by way of greeting. They were, apparently, to welcome Inez back, although why they should, Victoria couldn't understand. It wasn't as though she had been missed.

Meanwhile Juan stood by, his languishment equally divided between Inez and Victoria. He would stay to dinner? Inez smiled at him, eliminating his admittedly weak objections. His parents were expecting him? A telephone call and all would be well. . . . He was not correctly dressed? Inez pooh-poohed it. Dinner during Rafael's absence was less formal and she was certain that neither Abuela nor Victoria would object to his pearl grey trousers and blue silk shirt.

Victoria, made suddenly conscious of much washed, faded hipster jeans and a tee-shirt that had seen better days, whisked herself off to the kitchen to inform Pilar of the increase in numbers. Pilar laughed uproariously at the thought of being upset by one or two extra persons for dinner. Five! She spread her hand, counting on her fingers and pantomiming a distraught chef counting portions. Ten! Both her hands flew up, she shook her head and mimed an explosion, but two? *Es nada!* It's nothing. Victoria departed upstairs moodily, hoping that Juan had transferred his callow devotion from herself to Inez.

A long, hot bath restored her perspective somewhat and when Maria had brushed, plaited and coiled up her long coppery hair, she felt more sure of herself. Maria was getting quite good at it, so it no longer hung down her back like a schoolgirl's, neither did it hang about her face making her look like an unkempt witch.

The black silk caftan was given another airing, her feet stuffed into gold sandals to match the caftan's gold embroidery, and she went along the corridor to collect Isabel. Together they entered the *sala* where Inez was dispensing sherry.

'Sweet for you, isn't it?' Inez's tone was honeyed and Victoria, surprised to find that she was no longer worried by Inez, smiled sweetly back.

'Yes, please. I like that one called Oloroso.' Inez gave a polite shudder, but Juan took a serious view.

'Much of our sales in Britain are of the Oloroso and other sweet sherries. Perhaps it is a regional taste, because of your lack of sunshine. You might need the sweetness that only the sun can give.'

'It's a good excuse,' Victoria chuckled as she sipped appreciatively. 'Most English people have a sweet tooth.'

'*Pobrecita*,' languished Juan in a Byronic manner, apparently not noticing Victoria's rather grim look. 'Poor little one' indeed! How dared he be sorry for her just because she had her arm in plaster and didn't like dry sherry!

'There's no need to feel sorry for me,' she was tart. 'Ask Inez, she'll tell you. I've got it made.' Her eyes sparkled dangerously, but it was no use. She sighed disgustedly. The stupid boy was evidently intent on making a fool of himself despite anything she could do or say. She toyed with the idea of inventing a headache and retiring, but hunger prevented her. Already she could detect mouthwatering smells and she didn't see why she should forego a good dinner when she was starving, just because of a silly youth.

She retreated behind Abuela and Isabel and started a conversation on the beauties of Navarre, the delights of riding around in her own little car and how much she and Isabel had enjoyed their informal picnics. Unfortunately, she became quite animated, her eyes glowed and she laughed a lot, and Juan's soulful black eyes became riveted upon her with a gaze of intense devotion that made her feel quite sick.

After dinner, Victoria escaped for a while on the pretext of putting Isabel to bed. The little girl was drooping on her feet and Victoria found to her relief that she could waste a lot of time at this task. She and Isabel played with a rubber duck in the bath, trying to drown it, and when the child was safely tucked up in bed, Victoria went on reading aloud in a soft voice long after Isabel's dark eyes had closed and her breathing had become easy and regular denoting sleep.

It was with something akin to reluctance that Victoria joined the others in the *sala*, first going to compliment Pilar on the excellence of the dinner. She sat sipping coffee and listening to Inez recounting her exploits in Pamplona, she supposed. When Rafael was absent, she noticed, Inez rarely spoke in English; Abuela was more considerate.

At eleven o'clock, when Juan Martinez still showed no sign of leaving, Victoria decided that, manners or not, she was going to bed. Accordingly, she said so, and Abuela laughed.

'I remember also when Spanish ladies *never* went to bed.' Her dry chuckle was a little like the rustle of dry autumn leaves. 'We retired, we withdrew, but we *never* went to bed, but it is a good idea, I think. I am also weary and Sancha will be waiting for me, dozing in a chair, which will be bad for her rheumatism, so. . . .' The old lady rose to her feet.

Inez turned blazing black eyes on Victoria. 'Surely you do not mean to leave before Juan has departed?' she enquired in an icy voice. 'You are the hostess!'

'I know,' Victoria was cheerful, 'but I'm also the in-valid and I must have my beauty sleep. Rafael will be home tomorrow.' She added this as an afterthought.

Inez tinkled a light, brittle laugh. 'Rafael—you expect him so soon? Oh, my dear Victoria, you do not re-member, Rafael never comes on time. Always he is delayed. At the last minute there is always some "little bit of business" which requires his personal attention.' Her voice which had begun in its usual honeyed tones developed a definite suggestiveness and Victoria found her hackles rising as much by this as by the mournful, compassionate expression that was plastered all over Juan's face. She kept a cheerful smile pinned to her lips with an effort.

'Infuriating of him, isn't it?' she smiled sweetly at Inez, 'but then Rafael is . . . Rafael. Goodnight, everybody,' and she extricated herself without further ado.

Once upstairs, she became aware of weariness. The fresh air in the afternoon, she thought as she undressed, yawning. Suddenly she felt too tired to bother, so she let her clothes lie as they fell and slid gratefully between the cool sheets, luxuriating in the soft touch of fine linen against her skin, her eyes closing almost immediately.

There was a door and behind it she could hear voices, familiar voices. She had only to open the door and there would be dear familiar faces to match the voices and then she would remember everything. In the infuriating fashion of dreams, the door was farther away than she thought, right down the far end of a long black passage. She hurried towards it, never seeming to get any closer to it. The passage was full of a soft sticky web which clung to her hands and face, holding her back, and the floor was equally soft and gluey so that she could not run. The Red Queen laughed.

'You'll have to run much faster than that,' she told Victoria, 'if you want to get anywhere.' Victoria found herself sobbing with fear and desperation. The door was so close now, she could reach it by stretching out her hand, but the Red Queen was holding her tightly about the waist.

'Let me go!' she cried, struggling to free herself, and sat upright in bed, tears wetting her face, the nightmare still about her. The arm was still about her too, only the Red Queen had Rafael's face, was Rafael.

Grief and disappointment overwhelmed her. He shouldn't be here! He should be miles and miles away.

If he hadn't been here, she would have opened the door and remembered. Her tears became tears of rage and frustration, and through them she surveyed him with something closely akin to hate.

'It's your fault, all your fault!' she choked, pummelling his chest with a small futile fist. 'You shouldn't be here, not until tomorrow. Why can't you come when you're supposed to? I nearly remembered and you stopped me. I hate you!'

His arm tightened about her, pulling her down relentlessly, back into bed. 'Stop struggling, Victoria, you will hurt yourself.'

'I don't care!' she blazed at him. 'I don't care about anything. I nearly remembered and you stopped me. I could kill you!'

'You have been having a bad dream, *querida*. Now wake up properly.' The deep voice was calm and soothing. 'Wipe the tears from your face and be reasonable.'

'I *am* reasonable. I was going to see. . . .' Her voice faded into a mumble as the dream faded from her grasp and reality came into focus. But although the dream had gone, her rage remained.

'What are you doing here now?' she demanded. 'You aren't expected until tomorrow. Wasn't there any "little bit of business" to keep you longer?'

'You have been talking to Inez.' He closed his eyes.

The bland indifference infuriated her. 'So! I've been talking to Inez. Is there any reason why I shouldn't?'

'None at all,' he said equably as if it didn't matter a jot. 'But it is not always wise to take every word that falls from her lips as the complete truth. Inez has a way of implying things without saying them. She is very good at it, and it would be also wise for you to remember that she is not a happy woman.'

'And whose fault is that?' she snapped back at him. 'You brought her here, didn't you? What did you

promise her to make her come?—because you must
know that she's bored. This isn't her sort of life at all.
She's sophisticated and beautiful, she likes meeting
people, having lots of friends. What can she do here?
She loathes the country, she despises the people, to her
they're either peasants or provincials. She'd be much
happier in Madrid where she could have a proper social
life with lots of dinner parties, the theatre, the opera
and friends of her own sort. Why do you keep her here
when you know that she's bored to death?'

His grey eyes opened and in the thin light, they were
hard and cold. 'You mistake, *señora*. I do not keep Inez
here, she can leave whenever she chooses, a thing which
she will do as soon as an advantageous situation arises.
The only thing I refuse to do is to open up her family's
mausoleum of a house in Madrid, and since she refuses
to live in any other house, she stays here. It is her
own choice.'

'Bully for you,' Victoria muttered half under her
breath. 'The complete male chauvinist pig!'

Her shoulders were grasped in firm hands and she
was shaken until her teeth rattled. 'You do not speak to
me so!' he ground out the words through stiff lips. 'If
you want a fight, *mi mujer*, you can have one. You are
behaving like a peevish child. You wake in a bad temper,
you storm at me because of a dream, you call me by
names which I can only assume are not polite and you
accuse me of being unkind to Inez. What next will you
find to fight about? Are you going to accuse me of the
things of which Inez accuses me? How many women am
I supposed to have seduced into my hotel beds this time?
Because if this is so, I will treat you as if you are the
disgruntled child you sound. I will. . . .'

'Beat me?' she spat the words at him. 'Big deal! You're
twice as big as I am, and what will that prove anyway,
except that you've probably got a lecherous past and a
bad conscience to go with it. You can't stop me thinking,

and if you lay one finger on me, I'll never speak to you again—and,' she sent off on an entirely different tack, 'I found my car which you hid from me *and* I've been driving it for the last three days, so there!' Almost she put out her tongue at him.

'I know, and I did not hide your car. What did you expect, that it should be waiting for you on the drive as I brought you home from hospital?'

'You know! How did you know?'

'Carlos told me. Each night I have telephoned Carlos and he has reported to me.'

'Oh!' Her squeal of outrage was muffled as she turned her head into the pillow. 'How dare you spy on me! You and Carlos. Why didn't you ring *me*? There wasn't any need for sneaky phone calls when I was asleep, I'd have told you.'

Rafael chuckled unexpectedly, pulling her back against him. 'Always I have thought that your English is a most expressive language. I must try to remember that. "Sneaky phone calls". *Querida*, let us stop this stupid quarrel. No matter what you think. . . .'

'You can't stop me thinking,' she interrupted triumphantly.

'Yes, I can, *mi esposa*. Would you like to try me?'

Inexorably, she was drawn down closer to him, his hand tangling in her hair and forcing her face up to his.

'That's not fair,' she whispered after a long silence. 'That's no way to settle anything.'

'No?' There was another long silence until he, most reluctantly, lifted his mouth from hers. 'I think it is a very good, very pleasant way of settling most things between us, don't you?'

Victoria sighed, her peevishness and bad temper dissipating under the coaxing caress of his hands and mouth. 'It might stop an argument,' she told him, 'but it would never settle it.'

'Stop it or settle it, what does it matter? Just so that

you cease uttering these waspish sentiments which fall so readily from your lips. You are behaving like a shrewish wife, and that I will not have. I landed at Dieppe very early this morning,' he glanced at his watch and corrected himself, 'very early yesterday morning, and I have driven from there with as much speed as I could manage. If you have no welcome for me, then let me sleep.' He closed his eyes firmly, saying in an exasperated tone, 'Go to sleep yourself, perhaps you will wake in a better temper.'

'Dieppe?' Again her small fist pummelled his chest. 'Have you been to England? What were you doing there?'

'Ah! So now you show some interest. I have spent three days in your cool, damp London arranging the sale and distribution of Señor Martinez's sherry.'

'Juan was here tonight,' she told him. 'He brought Inez back from Pamplona and she invited him to dinner.'

'The least she could do, as he brought her back,' he murmured in her ear. 'And does the Young Lothario still make calves eyes at my wife?'

'I'm afraid so,' Victoria giggled. 'He just sits and moons. Tonight was a bit better, though, he had Inez to moon at as well.' She closed her eyes and turned on her side.

'My welcome first,' Rafael whispered, pulling her round to face him.

Sighing, she relaxed. It wasn't any use trying to fight him. Against his mouth she told him so. 'I can't hope to win,' she added, 'not against brute force. I'm thinking of using feminine guile.'

'Please demonstrate,' he demanded, his mouth serious. 'I thought it was a quality absent in you. I would like to see some of this feminine guile of yours.'

Very gently, almost sadly, she lowered her head to kiss a corner of the mouth so close to her own. It was asking for trouble, she knew, and she moaned softly as her eyes closed and her body moulded itself against his.

'This is guile, *querida*? You should use it more often.'

Much, much later she realised that he had explained nothing, nor had he apologised for anything, but somehow it no longer seemed to matter very much. She let her hand slide over his shoulder and across the smooth skin of his back, feeling the bone and muscle under the flesh. She shivered against him and he stirred sleepily, his arm tightening about her, pulling her even closer.

Why didn't it matter? she asked herself, and lay staring into the dim light that crept through the windows, unable to accept the answer. She was *not* in love! This was just sex. That was an unpleasant thought and her face flamed in the semi darkness. Rafael was very good at it and it was no use being embarrassed or blinking at the truth. She was a normal female, wasn't she? Hadn't he spoken about 'pleasurable nights' when he had brought her home from hospital? One didn't have to be in love for that. A deep sadness overwhelmed her and she felt tears sliding under her eyelids at the thought. She would very much have liked him to be in love with her—but of course, that was quite impossible.

CHAPTER SIX

THE September sun shone through the breakfast room windows. It was going to be another hot day, but already the evenings were growing chilly and a little cool, and damp breezes blew in from the Bay of Biscay. Victoria had been at the Casa for nearly six weeks.

Last week they had taken Isabel down to the small convent boarding school in Pamplona, to start the winter term. Jeans and tee-shirts had been put away and Isabel had appeared in a smart grey dress with a demure white collar. Victoria had been upset at the idea of sending the little girl to a boarding school, but Rafael had proved adamant. Her arguments, little rages and downright sulks had bounced off his implacable determination. His daughter was well enough to go, therefore go she would! The company of other girls of her own age would be good for her, the discipline of school life would be good for her. In fact, everything would be good for her. Victoria accepted defeat with a bad grace and Isabel went to school.

Now, outwardly sedate, she surveyed her husband across the breakfast table while she thoughtfully nibbled at a piece of toast. All his attention was being given to the letters he was reading and his dark face was expressionless. Austere, she thought; she couldn't tell what was going on behind that face. Who was it who had said, 'A mystery wrapped up in an enigma'? She couldn't remember, but whoever it was must have met somebody very like Rafael Sebastian Alvarez.

Enigmatic was a better word than austere, her thoughts ran on. 'Austere' sounded rather monkish, and there was nothing remotely monkish about her husband.

She envisaged him in a black suit and a white frilly shirt, a black string tie and a wide black hat, playing poker on a Mississippi paddle steamer. She wished she knew him a little better, knew what made him tick. Come to that, she wished she knew him a little. That would do for starters. She sighed and reached for the coffee pot.

'Something is wrong, Victoria?' He was putting the last letter tidily back in its envelope. 'You are not happy?'

'Of course there's something wrong,' she sighed again. 'I'm not unhappy, but I'm not happy either. You couldn't expect me to be, could you?' The effect of this rather muddled speech was to cause his face to become severe.

'That is not completely true, I think, *niña*, for I know there are times when you are very happy indeed.'

Victoria felt a warm flush spread over her whole body and gazed intently down at the contents of her coffee cup, willing the hot colour to go away. Desperately she wished for just a small part of Inez's ivory and shell pink self-possession. Taking a deep breath and mustering a small measure of sangfroid, she raised her head, hazel eyes steady as she looked at him.

'That wasn't fair,' she told him in a severe little voice. 'You're talking about bed and things like that, aren't you?'

His infrequent laugh annoyed her with its sheer amusement. '*Si*, I talk about "bed and things like that".' He parodied her tone. 'You sound ridiculous, *querida*, when you speak so. Like a well brought up schoolgirl from one of your so-English schools. One who speaks only of hockey sticks and netball.'

'So I'm ridiculous, am I?' she blazed momentarily. 'Because I don't like talking about certain things? If that's the way you think, you shouldn't have married me. I *can't* talk about private things, not even when they're private things I've shared with you. They're not for talking about—and anyway, you're just changing the subject. I want my memory back, something to look back on. I want to know that I did exist before I came to Spain. All I get from you is soothing syrup. Is there something you don't want me to remember?'

'No, Victoria. I just wish you to progress slowly, as the doctors have advised. They all advised that you should not be prompted, that you should remember for yourself. It would have been very easy for me to have invented a past for you—do you not trust me?'

'Ye-es.' Even to her own ears, she sounded doubtful. 'Yes, I suppose I do, but that's not the point, is it? I want to know about *me*! I *need* to know about me.'

'Then if that is what you want, that you shall have. Go and get ready now.' Rafael pushed back his chair and stood up. Immaculate as ever, she thought. Not a spot or wrinkle marred the pristine whiteness of his fine linen shirt, not a hair was out of place. She glanced down at her own small person in a self-congratulatory way; she didn't look too bad herself.

She eyed her brown trousers with pleasure. She had put on a little weight since coming from hospital and her clothes were fitting very nicely nowadays. Her cream shirt looked cool and becoming and upstairs, ready to put on, was a suede jerkin that matched the colour of her trousers. For today was *the* day. Today her plaster was coming off. One more chain removed, she told herself. She would be able to bathe properly, dress herself, wear tights, even do her own hair. Through her haze of mild jubilation she heard his voice.

'During the drive down to San Sebastian I will tell you what I know of you. After we have visited the hospital, we will have lunch and talk of what can be done to help you—but one thing, *señora*, you will understand. You are my wife. I did not force you into marriage, you came willingly, and whatever happens, you will remain my wife. That is understood? What is mine remains mine.'

'You speak as if I was one of your possessions!' she flared.

'Possession, *querida*, is like a sword. It has two edges, it cuts both ways.' There was a wry, rather sombre note in his deep voice.

'What's that supposed to mean?' Her tone was belligerent.

A dark grey, unfathomable gaze slanted down at her. 'Some little thing for you to think about, Victoria.'

Half an hour later, he started speaking while manoeuvring the car around two cyclists and a bullock cart.

'You came, as I said, a year ago. Isabel had been ill. She needed somebody to give her a little tuition and companionship. I had tried several Spanish ladies, but they were not suitable. They had about them a seriousness, a formality which I did not wish for. I wanted Isabel to learn to laugh again, to enjoy life in her limited way. There was a Frenchwoman,' his mouth curved in a reminiscent smile. 'She was worse than the others. She saw my daughter as some sort of infant prodigy to be stuffed with knowledge as a fowl is stuffed. No—for Isabel, I wanted somebody different, young enough to play with her, old enough to help her regain her confidence, overcome her enforced loneliness and the apathy into which she had sunk. So I put the matter in the hands of my London agent.'

'Why haven't you told me all this before?' Victoria looked at his profile. 'It might have helped, didn't you think of that?'

'As I said before, the doctors advised against it.' She could see the corner of his mouth drawn in tight. 'You wanted to remember so badly, they feared you would build up a fairy tale on the little I could tell you.' He took his eyes from the road momentarily to look at her. 'Do you wish me to continue?'

'You can't very well stop now,' she protested. 'You haven't even come to *me* yet.'

'Very well then, don't interrupt! My London agent found you—he advertised. You were a young graduate who wished to teach but had been unfortunate in not finding a post in a school. It was arranged that you should come here for one year. You know how that ended! You were young, gay and uncomplicated and for an English girl of twenty-three years, extremely innocent. That, of course, was an important requisite.' He smiled down at her. 'Intelligence, virtue and a happy disposition, they were obvious to anybody. Your virtue, that was obvious to me. Therefore your past is of no importance to me. It is of the future I think, as you should be thinking. But this past of yours—you have evidently become obsessed with it, and this I cannot understand.'

She stole another glance at the strong profile beside her, the beaklike arrogant nose and the firm line of his jaw. 'No, I don't suppose you do understand, you couldn't be expected to. You know who you are, you know everything about yourself.' She choked back a spasm of self-pity. 'You're a complete person, I'm not, I'm only half alive. It's wonderful looking into the future if you can ignore the past, but I want to know what I'm ignoring. I want to be sure there's nothing nasty there, waiting to jump out on me when I'm least expecting it. Why, somebody might come up to me one day and say "Hello, Victoria" with a knowing sort of leer and I'd not even know. After all, I'm not exactly the frigid type, am I?' She looked at him anxiously.

His shout of laughter made her start. 'No, Victoria, not frigid,' he choked on mirth, 'but if anybody should—er—leer at you, refer them to me. I am something of an expert in the matter of your virtue.'

His wife turned a glacial eye on him. 'Your sort of expertise is nothing to boast about,' she remarked with asperity, after which she sank back in her seat and kept silent while Rafael negotiated the traffic of San Sebastian.

There was no delay at the hospital; his own doctor was waiting for them, another dark, plump, little man introduced to Victoria as Dr Garcia. He reminded her of Dr Sanchez at the other hospital. She had liked Dr Sanchez, so she greeted Dr Garcia with a dazzling smile and went off happily with a well starched nurse to have the plaster cut off and an X-ray taken of her arm and wrist, all at a speed approximating that of light.

There were times, she ruminated, when Rafael's filthy rich arrogance paid handsome dividends!

On her return, she flicked a quick glance at him and bit back a grin of delight. In the very short time they had been in the hospital he had collected the inevitable retinue about him. A very superior Sister was hanging on each word that he uttered, a young and pretty nurse was gazing at him, eyes glazed with devotion, while two elderly doctors, like Tweedledum and Tweedledee, gave him a comprehensive duet of do's and don'ts regarding the Señora's arm. Another little nurse came hurrying with the X-ray film, which was immediately illuminated for his edification and the healed and healing bits of bone pointed out to him. His smile of thanks sent the little nurse walking backwards into a doorpost.

It wasn't fair, decided Victoria, that so much masculine charm should be wrapped up in one male package. Herself merely the patient and therefore ignored, she had plenty of time to observe the despicable way Rafael used that charm to get his own way—even so, she had to admit that he was a very attractive parcel and a glow spread through her. He was *her* parcel! Ruefully, she inspected as much of her own packaging as she could manage and came to the conclusion that most people would say, as she had said herself, she'd got it made.

Lunch was a very protracted affair. She had been led

firmly away from anything that vaguely resembled a seafood restaurant. Today was lush and plush day, they were in the dining room of a very top-drawer hotel surrounded by soft-voiced, silent-footed waiters, velvet upholstery, snowy napery and sparkling crystal.

Today there would be no animated discussion on the merits of various dishes; she would not point at one and say 'I'll have that'. No, today she found herself escorted to the ladies' powder room as if it was an understood thing that no lady coming into this dining room from outside was fit to be seen. Victoria washed her hands, renovated her make-up and smoothed her hair, regretting that there would be no monstrous jug of Sangria on the table with lovely pieces of peach and chunks of orange floating amid the ice cubes. Today, Rafael would pore over a menu and a wine list while a stately maître d'hôtel would agree fawningly with every choice he would make.

It was no use, she told her reflection in the mirror of the powder room; she did not appreciate properly the things that money and breeding bought. She was a peasant at heart, as Inez had intimated on more than one occasion. When she was happy, she laughed; when she was not, she threw things about! But not today. She nodded to herself in the mirror. Today, you'll behave yourself, my girl. Sedately she returned to the table, filled with so many good intentions that she could have paved the road to Hell alone and unaided.

Lunch was delicious but protracted. Spanish waiters are not noted for speed, and here their speed was reduced to a dignified slow march. There was no rush to get the soup on the table before it went off the boil, so to speak. Here, a trolley came bearing the tureen, gently simmering on its own little meths burner, right up to the table, and the soup was ladled directly on to the plates. Then, of course, one had to wait until all danger of scalding one's mouth had passed. When the

soup was finished, nobody came hotfoot to remove the
plates, replacing them with others. Adequate time was
left for conversation, in fact conversation was a necessity
to fill in the waiting time.

'Do I have a passport? What I mean is, did I keep my
own when I married you or did you have me put on
yours or whatever it is that you do in Spain?' Victoria
found herself practically whispering the question.

'You kept your British passport, *querida*. How else
could you have gone to Lourdes as you did? Lourdes is
in France, you had to go through the border control.
As to where it is now——' Rafael shrugged his elegant
shoulders eloquently. 'In ashes, I presume, together
with everything else in the car when it burned at
Roncevalles.'

'You aren't going to forgive me for that, not properly,
are you? Oh, I know you keep saying that it doesn't
matter, but you are holding it against me.' Her mouth
was mutinous and she kept her eyes firmly on the tablecloth as she continued in an angry mutter, 'I know I
cost you a car, but. . . .'

'The loss of the car is of no importance.' Impatiently
he looked at her. 'I have told you that before. You will
please not mention it again. Why do you ask for your
passport?'

'Because it would say where I was born and when,'
she explained as she would to a child. 'If I knew that, I
could get a copy of my birth certificate and then I could
go and trace myself right from the start. It would take
some time, but I'd do it.'

'I have contact with a firm of enquiry agents in
London,' Rafael offered helpfully. 'They are often used
in business. One wishes to know the reliability of
customers. My agents would be much quicker.' He
slanted a charming smile down at her.

Full of outrage, Victoria told him just what she
thought of enquiry agents. 'I dont want them!' she said

forcefully. 'I've heard about them. They sneak about in dirty raincoats and they keep tatty old files in tatty old safes in disgusting back-street offices. Anybody can break in and steal them, even children, and then the files are found on rubbish dumps and newspaper men run Sunday serials on people's private lives. I'm not having sleazy little men ferreting and burrowing in *my* past!' She looked at him defiantly. 'Any ferreting to be done, I'll do myself!' A quick glance at his face acquainted her with the fact that her burst of independence was, to say the least, ill advised.

Coldly and courteously, he explained, 'Your ideas on enquiry agents are derived from the cinema and television programmes, neither of which give a true picture. Most enquiry agents are no more addicted to dirty raincoats than any other part of the population, and any firm which I employ is eminently respectable, even if some of the clothes worn cannot be termed haute couture. Nor do they inhabit grubby back-street offices!' He snorted and looked down his arrogant beak of a nose.

'Furthermore,' and there was a nasty glint in his eyes as he continued, 'you will not be allowed to go ferreting anywhere without *my* permission!' Her gasp of outrage was met with a formal chilliness and the cool statement, 'You are now, to all intents and purposes, a Spanish wife, and while in the northern parts of the American continent and in Europe, Women's Lib is in the ascendant, this is Spain, and here,' he gave her a nasty look, 'a husband's commands to his wife are the next best thing to Holy Writ!'

These archaic views caused Victoria to splutter over a glass of sweet white wine, but collecting herself and matching cold courtesy with an equally cool and courteous defiance, she told her Spanish husband, through petal-like lips stiff with anger, that he was behaving like Neanderthal man. 'I won't put up with it!' Her eyes glittered. 'I'm not a chattel and I'll go to England if I want to.'

The nasty gleam in his eyes increased. 'Try to do so, *señora*. Without a passport, you will get no farther than the passport control in any direction.'

At this, Victoria subsided. His argument was irrefutable and full of logic and she discovered, much to her surprise, that anger had given her a wonderful appetite. She sank her white teeth into a piece of steak in a very vicious fashion, meanwhile thinking up schemes that would make life uncomfortable for this relic from the age of masterful men.

Quite by chance, from the hotel window she noticed, swinging gently in the still warm sea breeze, a sign that said '*Peluquero*'. A hairdresser! Her eyes gleamed with a venomous glow, the dark green of emeralds. This would do for a start. Without stopping to think of the consequences, she announced that now she was free of the plaster, she might as well further lighten her person. 'I'll have my hair cut off. These last weeks have demonstrated to me the nuisance value of long hair, so I'll take the opportunity of visiting a hairdresser. I rather think I fancy a short, boyish style, something I can run a comb through. . . .' She smiled at Rafael sweetly, her eyes wide, innocent and limpid.

She proceeded no farther than that. A long-fingered brown hand came out to cover her smaller one where it lay on the table. To anybody who might have been watching, it was a lovely, loverlike gesture which, coupled with two pairs of eyes, one of hazel, the other of dark, stormy grey gazing into each other, positively oozed romance and 'The Voice that breathed o'er Eden'. That was the impression to be gathered by the incurious viewer. To Victoria, the handclasp was no warm, gentle gesture. After only a second, his vicelike grip made her wonder if she would need to return to the hospital for another plaster to mend crushed and broken bones in her hand. Some colour left her face and she bit her lip hard, but her eyes remained on his, defiant even if there were tears at the back of them.

'You will *not* have your hair cut. I like it as it is, and therefore that is the way it will stay!'

'It's *my* hair,' she choked back her outrage, 'and I'll do what I like with it!'

He agreed with her politely. 'Yes, as you say, it is your hair, but I have to look at it and therefore it will not be cut off. Furthermore, if you are so set on making a scene in a public place, I think you should remember one thing. This is Spain, and your Spanish, even after a year, is quite deplorable. If you continue to be so aggravating, you'll get your scene, and you won't like it because I shall make it. And I promise you, Victoria, it will be bigger and better than anything you can imagine.'

This threat was accompanied by another loverlike squeeze of her hand which brought tears to her eyes and reduced her to silence, or nearly so.

'Male chauvinist pig!' She made the remark in a low thrilling whisper with a sweet smile on her face. 'Bully!' That was the final shot in her locker.

Rafael nodded calmly at her. 'Of course! You are quite correct in your reading of my character. I am very proud of these qualities you appear to find so upsetting, Victoria. It is no part of my make-up to be any woman's lapdog!'

Somewhere during this loverlike exchange of compliments, all desire for a new hairdo left her. She hadn't really wanted it anyway. For some reason, she considered her hair to be one of her few assets. She was short and her face, while quite pleasant, would never launch a thousand ships, or even one. She had quite nice eyes and so on, but the sum total of the single items added up to a very ordinary whole. Her hair set her apart, she was proud of it, and she admitted to herself that she had only mentioned having it cut because she thought it would annoy Rafael. All the same, he *was* an arrogant pig and she felt quite justified.

The drive back to the Casa was accomplished in near-silence. He slanted a faint smile down at her, a smile that was mostly a grimace of exasperation.

'You are behaving like a sulky child.' He said it with a kind of lordly contempt.

Victoria found the remark beneath contempt. She was behaving beautifully. Her eyes might blaze green fire, but her voice was cool and precise, her grammar elegant and her vocabulary wide and comprehensive without the use of one small swear-word. 'You're a relic,' she told him in a beautifully modulated voice. 'A relic of bygone days. You should at least attempt to bring yourself up to date. The age of masterful men has passed, and there is now equality of the sexes. I can only imagine that your mother spoilt you when you were young and your father encouraged you in your high-handed ways.' She was behaving very well under intense provocation, she thought, and sat for the rest of the journey, lips folded tightly in case the hot words that filled her and raged around her brain burst out of their own volition; and she was *not* sulking.

It was true that she felt very ill used. Her request had been reasonable and although phrased more as a statement of intent than a request, it did not warrant his high-handed attitude or the gross brutality of his squeezing her hand until it was all she could do not to scream the place down. Furthermore, on leaving the hotel, he had grasped her arm in a punishing grip that would be certain to leave bruises. Tonight she would wear a sleeveless dress for dinner, the white one which he had bought in San Sebastian, and everyone should see how she had been treated. She peeped at her arm, trying to see if the bruises were forming, and felt a definite sense of satisfaction as she observed the dark imprints of his fingers. By tonight they should be a lovely purple. Good! She maintained her outward appearance of calm disdain, while inwardly fulminating against men in general and this one in particular, and she kept her hands tightly clasped in case one of them should get loose and deal him a ringing slap.

Once in the house, she walked upstairs and shut herself in the bedroom. There was no key in the door, so she was denied the pleasure of locking herself in. There was, however, a key in the bathroom door, so she locked herself in there. After giving way to a storm of weeping and feeling much better for it, she drew a bath, a deep, hot one, and lost no time in immersing herself, revelling in the fact that there was no longer a great lump of concrete on her arm which had to be kept dry. She extended the bath time for as long as possible, emerging into the bedroom nearly an hour later, flushed with the heat of the water, a large towel wound sarongwise about her damp body and another smaller towel, turbanlike, on her head. She had washed the hair in dispute and could now sit for another hour or so drying it. She hoped it would make her late for dinner.

For the remainder of that day and all the next one, Victoria had about her the hard glitter of a diamond. This was in part due to the fact that her husband did not seem to realise that he had transgressed or feel obliged to apologise for his boorish and brutal behaviour, and in part to the fact that Victoria was at heart a reasonable and fair-minded young woman. Each time her temper cooled and a sense of humour and fair play seemed to be in the ascendant, she was forced to seek an unoccupied room and go over again, step by step and word for word, the quarrel in San Sebastian. This was necessary to maintain her sense of ill-usage and her malicious determination to be as awkward as possible.

One thing emerged from all this. Inez started to look

at her with a dawning respect. Her black eyes were no longer hostile and once or twice Victoria surprised a small smile on the red, luscious lips. Of course, this state of affairs could not last, and after the thirty-six hours were up Victoria decided magnanimously to forgive her husband, thus proving her moral superiority. That he quite evidently didn't feel in any need for forgiveness worried her not a bit. Her temper was of the instant variety and to keep it up for any long period of time put a strain on her.

Rafael seemed not to notice either her bad temper or her recovery. He was unfailingly good-tempered and ignored the catty remarks she felt impelled to make now and then.

At night she had buttoned her pyjamas right up to her chin and lay very still on the extreme edge of her side of the bed. She was completely demoralised, on waking, to find herself on enemy territory and all her pyjama buttons undone. She was very confused and castigated herself as a sexy little idiot. The second time this happened, she smiled ruefully and snuggled down more comfortably in Rafael's arms with one hand and arm clasping him close.

A week later they drove down to Pamplona on the Friday afternoon to collect Isabel from school. The weekend, plus a couple of saints' days, made it a worthwhile break. As the car drew into the entrance Victoria saw a row of expectant, curious faces at a downstairs window, but when she waved to them, they all disappeared as if they had been erased by a duster. Isabel was waiting for them, sitting primly in a frigid little room, her black curls and small face nearly eclipsed by a wide-brimmed felt hat. A navy blue half-belted coat covered her small form and her little hands were decently covered with navy woollen gloves, the thumb of one glove looking distinctly soggy. Isabel must have been waiting for some time.

On seeing them, the child scrambled down from the chair and flung herself at Victoria, black curls bobbing under the eclipsing hat and black eyes sparkling with delight. A torrent of unanswerable questions spilled from her lips and, wisely, Victoria made no attempt to answer them; they were mostly superfluous anyway.

Rafael was greeted in a more restrained manner, but no less lovingly. He teased his daughter gently on how much she had grown in the last two weeks, smiling with warm eyes and gentle mouth at the little face close to his own. Victoria caught her breath as she watched them. How many faces did this man have—this man who was her husband?

Mentally she listed them, the ones she already knew. Cool indifference, cold courtesy, chill arrogance, remote amusement—that one was the one he kept for her! And then there was this kind, compassionate one he had for Isabel. She closed her eyes and shivered slightly as she recalled the memory of his olive-dark face set hard, eyes glittering and nostrils pinched with contained rage, as she had seen it across the dining table in San Sebastian. Isabel would never see that face, she hoped.

The little girl chattered gaily on the back all the way home. How she was going to put on her jeans and go to see her pony and have a grand tour of inspection.

'I am sure that there must be some kittens by this time,' she crinkled up her face. 'Pilar says the cat is always having kittens and I haven't seen any for months. The mother of Margarita and Mercedes, who are my school friends, has a little black dog, a poodle. It wears a collar covered in sparkly stones and has a red ribbon tied in the hair on top of its head, it sleeps on a velvet cushion on the bottom of their mother's bed and it only eats chicken livers and fish boiled in milk.' Isabel sounded suitably awed and glanced at her father expectantly.

'No dog is going to sleep on my bed,' Rafael growled, 'with or without a velvet cushion.'

'Oh no!' Isabel agreed with him quickly. 'Perhaps it might get off its cushion and come to lie beside you, and then you might think it was Victoria and cuddle it. But a kitten, a very small kitten, could sleep on a bed if there was only one person in that bed. My bed?' she finished hopefully.

Victoria turned the suggestion down, but diplomatically. 'It might wake in the night and be frightened. It might want its mother. I think a kitten would be happier sleeping with other kittens in a furry tangled heap.'

Isabel thought that Victoria was very clever to know such things.

There were kittens in plenty, the kitchen cat had five bundles of black fur cosily tucked into her side in the broom closet. There were more outside in the stables, but the stable cat was half wild; she hid her kittens from Isabel's searching eyes and growled fiercely when the little girl went prying. The kitchen cat was more accommodating. She viewed her offspring's unsteady progress about the broom cupboard with equanimity, although if one wandered too far, she lethargically rose, caught the offender and carried it back to the box where she pinned it down with a firm paw and cleaned it thoroughly to remove any contamination it might have picked up on its travels. Isabel spent every available minute with the kittens, and Victoria, seeing her so happily engaged, regretted the necessity of her returning to the school and said so.

Rafael was not sympathetic. '*Querida*,' he sounded exasperated, 'the kittens will be kittens for only a short time, they will soon grow into cats. We cannot suspend Isabel's education because of them. They will still be here the next time she comes for a weekend, but after that, Pilar will have to give them away or we should swiftly be overrun with cats.'

Victoria gave way, albeit grudgingly. The weekend gave her no time for introspection. There was a picnic planned for the afternoon, but before that, there was a solemn conference with Abuela.

Isabel had been commanded by one of her teachers to begin a new piece of embroidery of her own design. She was to take it back to school with her and marks would be given for originality and neatness. Like any other eight-year-old, Isabel knew definitely what she did not want to do. She did not wish to make a handkerchief with an initial in the corner, Margarita and Mercedes were doing that, neither did she wish to make a cushion cover with a wreath of flowers, nor an embroidered pinafore. The trouble seemed to be that she also did not know what she did want.

Abuela sent her off to the small sitting-room with orders to observe everything and possibly find a piece she wished to copy. Ten minutes later Isabel returned in triumph and excitement, in her hand a small picture frame which contained, under glass, an old Victorian sampler either of English or American origin. There was a delightful cross-stitch border which enclosed a house, a tree and a misshapen dog with, underneath the legend, 'There's no Place Like Home'. Underneath this was embroidered, also in cross-stitch, 'Emma Collins, aged Nine years. Her work'.

Isabel did not like the tree, the house or the dog. Her sampler would be different. Meanwhile, Abuela supplied the silks and wool and Sancha was sent to find a piece of suitable linen and the cross-stitch border was begun under Abuela's watchful eye.

On Monday, Rafael, Isabel and Victoria left very early for Burgos. It was a long journey, but the road from San Sebastian to Bilbao was good and at Bilbao they turned south on the E3 to Vittoria and their destination. Victoria was disappointed in Burgos. She had expected somewhere with white walls, red pantiled roofs and brilliant sunshine, but Burgos was grey, windy and very cold.

'Over there,' Rafael gestured north and west, 'is Leon. It is not a province which is popular with tourists as it has typical Biscayan weather. The forests there are quite dense and I have heard, though I have never seen for myself, that there are still wolves.'

'And did you know,' Isabel rattled off another history lesson, 'that once, long ago, the Pope put a ban on Leon. Nobody was allowed to be born or get married or die for many years. I don't think I would have liked that.' Her small face crumpled with unpleasant thoughts. 'There wouldn't have been any weddings or birthdays or babies. I like babies. When are you going to have a baby, Victoria?'

Victoria gulped, swallowed half a sandwich and broke into a violent fit of coughing.

'I don't know,' she gasped when she had enough breath. 'I hadn't thought about it, but now that you've mentioned it, I suppose we should consider it.' She tried to keep her voice normal, to steady it, to speak matter-of-factly. It was difficult, but she congratulated herself that she managed it.

Isabel was delighted. 'All my friends at school,' she informed them beamingly, 'have brothers or sisters, sometimes both. Could you have one very soon, because I've half promised Margarita and Mercedes that they can come and see it and they are leaving school next year because their mother is going to live in Zaragoza. I've told Sister Teresa about it. Perhaps, though,' Isabel was considerate, 'it would be better to wait until I am a little bigger because then I could look after it for you. It would be quite small and I'm sure I could manage.'

'You have discussed this with Sister Teresa?' Rafael's voice sounded as if he had been strangled.

'Oh yes! But she's not much help, Papa. She says the same thing every time. "These things are with God!"' Isabel sighed.

Victoria bundled picnic things back into the car.

'We don't want to be late back, do we?' she said
chattily. 'It's a long drive and already it's nearly four
o'clock.' She hunted through her mind for a diversion.
'There's your piece of embroidery, have you thought of
what to put in the middle yet?'

As an effort at turning the conversation, this proved
very effective.

'Words would be nice,' Isabel smiled sunnily, 'and
English words would be even nicer.' So, on the long
journey home, Victoria dredged up every quotation she
could bring to mind. Each one considered and rejected
as being either too long or too short or the meaning was
too obscure. After over an hour, Victoria sat, empty of
inspiration, still willing but numb and drained.

Rafael then suggested that they should try
Shakespeare. 'A very famous English poet,' he informed
his daughter.

'Gather ye rosebuds while ye may,' Victoria quoted.
'But that's not Shakespeare. It's by another English poet
of about the same time, Robert Herrick.'

Isabel was entranced. There could be rosebuds around
the words and she could do rosebuds, therefore the
choice of poet was immaterial. Still talking sleepily of
rosebuds and samplers, she ate her supper and stumbled
into bed, asleep as her head touched the pillow.

Inez greeted them in the *sala* before a rather late
dinner. Tonight there was no catty remark about
Victoria's preference for sweet sherry and wines. Inez
must be mellowing, thought Victoria, and smiled at her,
rather surprised to have the smile returned in quite a
warm way. The chill in the air had woken Abuela's
rheumatism, for she moved with more difficulty and was
decidedly crotchety. She refused coffee and accepted
Rafael's arm to help her to her room, a sign of weakness
which she covered up by tart comments on his lack of
conversation at dinner.

Inez, lounging gracefully in the *sala*, looked

across at Victoria.

'You seem to have made quite a conquest,' she drawled, examining the toes of her evening slippers. 'Juan Martinez—he was here again today, just before lunch—was desolated to find you not at home. You must not be cruel to him, little cousin, he is very young.'

'He is also very stupid!' Victoria bit back the remark that no woman in her right senses would exchange Rafael for a callow, lovesick idiot like Juan. To say things like that might not be good for her husband's ego; that ego was big enough already. What little she had suffered from Juan's devotion she had found embarrassing and boring. 'I wish he'd find himself a nice girl of his own age.'

Rafael, who had that moment re-entered the *sala*, paused in the act of pouring his coffee.

'You have forgotten again, *querida*, that this is Spain and that Juan comes of a good and wealthy family. A number of "nice" girls will undoubtedly be found for him, if one has not been selected already, and at the right time he will inevitably marry. But until then, the free-and-easy attitudes current in England do not apply. Things are not as strict as they were years ago and I expect parties of young people might be permitted, providing that they were suitably chaperoned by a set of parents, but a freer type of relationship would tend to damage a girl's chances of an advantageous marriage.' He smiled wryly down at Victoria's recumbent figure. 'Therefore any girl's parents would be very careful of their daughter, because a marriage with Juan Martinez would be very advantageous indeed.'

Victoria goggled at him. 'It sounds archaic,' she scowled at her husband. 'And meanwhile, Juan can go around making sheep's eyes at older women, embarrassing them, because that's what he does to me!' She slammed down her coffee cup and scrambled to her feet.

'It's not civilised. I know it's your way, but it's not civilised!'

'It will not be for long,' Inez smiled comfortingly, and Victoria caught back a gasp of surprise. 'Just before Christmas he goes to Jerez,' Inez resumed her contemplation of her toes. 'To his uncle, who has the task of training him in the wine business. Export, I think,' she said musingly. 'I cannot imagine Juan coping with vines. Until then, I think you will have to suffer.'

Victoria had no intention of suffering. She very much hoped that well before Christmas, young Juan would have found himself another object of devotion. She hoped that he would cast all his sheep's eyes elsewhere, at Inez perhaps, who was well worth looking at!

She said as much to Rafael as she sat plaiting her hair before getting into bed, and he frowned slightly as if something unpleasant had been waved under his arrogant nose.

'What's wrong?' she asked. 'Have I said something I shouldn't? I'm not suggesting for one minute that Inez. . . .'

'No, Victoria, it is I who have not been thinking clearly. You spoke of him making sheep's eyes at older women and I accepted it, but I do not think he looks upon you as an older woman.' He walked across to the dressing-table and picked up her hairbrush, examining it without seeing it, his eyes hidden behind the heavy lids and curling lashes. 'I look at you now and I see a very young woman, little more than a girl.' He raised his eyes to meet hers in the mirror.

'Why, thank you, kind sir.' She swept him a mocking curtsey, the old green velvet robe spread, revealing cotton pyjamas of a strictly utilitarian variety. She grinned at him and evading his outstretched hand, slipped into bed. She was just drifting into sleep when his voice brought her back to full consciousness.

'When Isabel returns to school, on Wednesday, is it

not?' she nodded at him wonderingly, 'I think we will take a little journey to England.'

'England!' Victoria almost shrieked her excitement. 'You've had my passport, then?'

'No, *pequeña*, but I can obtain Spanish papers for you very quickly.' Then he added magnanimously, 'While you are in England, you can apply for a replacement of your British passport.'

'Is this because of tracing me, or to remove me from the amorous young Juan Martinez?'

'Both, of course, my Victoria. I have always liked killing two birds with one stone.' He pulled her close against him, kissed her thoroughly and bade her go to sleep.

'Go to sleep? Don't be ridiculous.' She yawned. 'How can I go to sleep now? England!' she sighed blissfully on another yawn, and her eyes closed as she slept.

CHAPTER SEVEN

EVEN in the shelter of the trees the hillside was cold, but Victoria felt little physical discomfort as she huddled in a blanket coat, seated on the short turf, her knees drawn up to her chin. She gazed with blank, unseeing eyes in the direction of the sea while the wind tore at her hair. She couldn't see the sea from where she was sitting, it was hidden by hills and was much too far away, and in any case she didn't particularly want to see it. The memories of a thirty-six-hour crossing of the Bay of Biscay from Southampton to Bilbao were uncomfortable in the extreme. They were also painful, and she preferred to forget them.

The heaving grey waters slipping past the sides of the ship had matched the heave in her stomach. She had spent most of the time on deck; the thought of entering the brightly lit cabin which smelled of hot engine oil had made her nausea worse and she had emerged from the voyage at Bilbao feeling only relief at being back on dry land. There was a lovely solid concrete wharf which remained firm under her feet and did not heave up and down, she could have gone down on her hands and knees and kissed it!

The journey had definitely upset her. She never wanted to see the sea again—or any of its denizens either, for that matter. The sight of even a cooked fish sent her retching from the table and she woke, covered in perspiration and fighting nausea, from dreams of sullen grey waves which reared and tumbled to engulf her.

It had all been a waste of time anyway. She and Rafael had flown to London, a dreadful journey because there was a strike among some part of the airport per-

sonnel and they had had an interminable wait, first at
Bordeaux and then again at Paris, which had made them
over a day late arriving in London. A faint grin crossed
her face. Even Rafael's arrogance and charm had not
met with success against a union. True, there had been
the usual flutter of airport officials to make them comfortable.

Not for Rafael and his wife a couple of seats in an
airport lounge crowded with other passengers, with
plastic packets of sandwiches and plastic mugs of coffee.
Oh no! Rafael smiled gently and a distraught recep-
tionist surrounded by clamouring would-be passengers
freed herself for a moment to call another less distraught
official who pondered the problem for two seconds
only before escorting them to a small room where it was
blessedly quiet and Victoria could sleep.

At Paris, they did not even stay in the airport. A taxi
was waiting to drive them to a small hotel, comfortable
and quiet. They had eaten a delicious meal and returned
just in time to hear their flight called.

Visiting Queen Mary's College had been worse than
useless. Her name was there in the records: Victoria
Plummer. B.A. Cum Laude; next of kin—None! That
was all. Nothing and nobody was familiar, and nobody
knew her.

They had motored down to Wickham in Hampshire
where she had lived with her aunt, but the little Georgian
house fronting on to what had been the town green and
was now a flat grey car park brought back no memories
at all. The grey headstone in the churchyard which
announced that Elizabeth Emily Plummer had died in
her sixty-seventh year in 1978, had left Victoria feeling
even more lost and lonely.

There had been an unutterable relief in turning to the
shelter of Rafael's arms, burying her face in his chest
when it was wet with rain and tears. Here was warmth
and comfort, and also recognition, and she clung to him

desperately. In England she had found nothing; it was as if she had never existed before she went to Spain, as if she had been born one day in late July, in a hospital outside Pamplona and aged twenty-three years. There was no warm family group to welcome her, only a green plot in this country churchyard and another plot, of which she had only a photograph in a bigger churchyard in Dundee where she had been born and where her parents had died when she was three years old. It was useless to go there; three-year-olds don't have much in the way of memory, and Wickham, which she should have remembered, did not ring a bell.

Her throat ached with the effort of choking back more tears as Rafael walked beside her back to the hired car. In its warm interior she let her head fall back against the headrest and closed her eyes.

'It's all been such a waste, such a dreary waste.' Tears coursed down her cheeks and her voice was reduced to a hoarse, stumbling whisper. Rafael swore comprehensively in Spanish and shook her.

'Not quite a waste,' he said flatly.

'Why not?' she demanded huskily. 'There's nothing here for me, is there? No family, nothing.' She looked at him gloomily. 'Did you know when we came? Yes, you did, didn't you? You've had your enquiry agents at work, that's why you wouldn't let me come alone, isn't it?'

'Yes,' his tone was astringent. 'In a way I knew—not everything, I admit. I did not have enquiry agents as you call them, but my London agent, the one who interviewed you, he keeps very comprehensive records, and he kept a detailed one of your interview. But if I had told you, even showed you a copy, you would not have believed me. Your head was stuffed full of romantic nonsense about a loving family and you would never have believed me if I had said that the only family you had was the one at the Casa.'

'And now you're gloating!' Victoria raised angry eyes

still wet with tears. 'No wonder that sometimes I hate you, you're always right! Nobody has any right to be as right as you are. You're worse than a computer!'

'And again, you are wrong. I brought you here, not to disillusion you but to try to make you remember. I thought that familiar scenes might stir something in you—this small town, the house where you lived for so long. But it was not so.' He reached forward to turn the ignition key. 'Now, I think that we will return home. We will have one day in London, I to attend to some business and you for some shopping, then we will go.' He flicked her a quick smile. 'By ship, I think. I do not care to be held up at airports.'

With an effort, Victoria dragged herself back to the present, to the cold hillside and the trees bending in the strong breeze. She shivered. At last she was feeling something, if only the cold. It was nearly a week since she had arrived home and she had been numb with grief until now. She had taken long solitary walks, avoiding company, sat alone at the bedroom window for hours looking but seeing nothing, not even the slow but perceptible change that heralded the end of summer. But grief cannot last for ever and, slowly but surely, she had found feeling creeping back.

This was the last day she would come and sit in this spot to sort things out. Now she was composed and quiet; she had at last come to terms with her life, this so odd life of hers that had begun in the middle instead of at the beginning. Perhaps she might never remember, but if she did, it would be a bonus. The dreadful feeling of isolation had vanished in a rush of common sense. She was not alone, she had a family of sorts, a Spanish one. Isabel, with her piquant little face, merry and serious by turns; Abuela, old and stern, sometimes crotchety but loving and understanding as well. There was Inez too, now that she knew her better. She had a beautiful home with friendly people, Pilar, Carlos, Maria, even little Carlota and the silent, earnest Renata, and last but not least, she had Rafael—or some part of him.

He had been so definite when he had brought her from the hospital. 'In your own home and among those who love you'. That was what he had said, and Victoria had wasted time yearning for a home, family and friends when they were right here under her nose all the time. And what of Rafael, the kingpin of it all? Did he love her? He'd never said so. Did she love him or was it just a matter of physical need. She hoped it wasn't as crude as that. There ought to be more to loving a person than the earthy side of it. Memories of nights in his arms brought a flush to her cheeks. Surely she couldn't have behaved in such an abandoned, wanton way if she didn't love him, could she?

She thought about this new problem; it wouldn't have been so bad if she could have had some sort of standard to measure her feeling by, but was there a yardstick for love? Her new problem and all it entailed remained with her as she rose to her feet and, clutching the loose coat about her, started on the walk back home.

The Casa was in a state of uproar when she pushed her way through the great door. Maria, Carlota and Renata were scurrying about, up and down stairs, in and out of rooms, hurrying to and fro and each one was adding another piece of luggage to the pile in the hall—a pile which threatened to assume gigantic proportions. Pilar was directing operations, waving a wooden spoon to emphasise her commands and shouting in a stentorian voice, a voice which drowned completely the light chatter of Maria and Carlota and nearly but not quite eclipsed the thin reedy pipe of Sancha, who was complaining loudly from the top of the stairs. Raquel, as became a newcomer, hurried in silence and kept well away from her aunt's brawny arm.

Victoria stood speechless, watching the running

figures and shocked into speechlessness by the appalling din. Whatever was going on? Whatever it was, her mouth tightened and she became indignant. It should go on no longer. She spoke, but her voice was lost in the hubub, so she picked up the felt-headed hammer lying on the table and delivered a violent blow to the big brass gong that hung on the wall above it. The brazen clamour reverberated through the hall, startling the excited women into silence.

'*Que pasa?*' she demanded. 'What's going on?'

Pilar, Maria and Sancha all started to speak at once, excitedly in Spanish, very fluidly and very fast. Victoria, who was still stumbling through Chapter Five of her very elementary Spanish primer, could understand about one word in a hundred, and bade them all be quiet. One person could do the talking, so she gestured at Maria whose English was quite reasonable. 'You,' she said, and heard for the first time a hint of authority in her own voice. 'Tell me, explain.'

Maria opened her mouth, but her explanation was forestalled by Inez, who came down the stairs at that moment. Inez in a suit of pale grey silk, a froth of fine lace about her neck and falling in a jabot between the lapels of her jacket. A mink coat was thrown carelessly about her shoulders and she stopped by the pile of luggage looked at it closely and frowned. 'Sancha,' she called, 'you've forgotten my dressing case. Fetch it at once, or must I do everything for myself?' She caught sight of Victoria and sauntered across the grey flagstones.

'I am leaving, little cousin.' Her red mouth had a twist to it that made it a bitter curve, but apart from that, the perfect, patrician features showed no expression, not even her eyes. Victoria looked around. Pilar and her daughters and the silent Raquel had vanished to their own domain and Sancha was toiling up the stairs, scolding reedily.

Victoria hesitated for only a second, then she crossed

to the nearest door and flung it open. 'In here,' she said, and there was a bite to the words. Inez raised her eyebrows and entered the room with an elegant shrug. Victoria closed the door behind them.

'Does Abuela know you're going?'

Inez snorted delicately down her well bred nose. 'Of course she knows. Oh, don't worry,' as she saw the frown gather between Victoria's eyes, 'she'll miss me as little as anyone else in this house. Perhaps even less than you will.'

'But why, and why now? Does Rafael know—have you told him?' There was concern in Victoria's voice.

'Why now? Because it suits me to go now, and why should I tell Rafael? I do not have to explain my actions to him, to you or to anybody.' Inez shrugged her mink closer about her shoulders and went to the door. With her hand on the knob she turned, looking back at Victoria with a slight smile.

'When you first came here, little cousin, I despised you—a silly little English girl with your vulgar red hair and your pathetic little body. I was wrong to do that. When Rafael married you and gave you my position as mistress here, I thought that I would hate you, but I found it almost impossible. Now that I am leaving, I think I like you. *Adios,* little cousin, come and see me when you are in Madrid.' An elegant gloved hand waved a slight farewell, then Inez hesitated, her dark eyes met Victoria's. 'Before I go, a word of warning. Will you take it, I wonder, from me?' Her eyebrows rose in a faint question. 'Juan Martinez—he is a spoilt child, a spoiled, vicious child. Have a care, little cousin.' The door closed gently behind her and she was gone. A delicate trace of a musky perfume lingered in the air for a moment, then that was gone too, leaving Victoria standing bemused and faintly regretful. She heard the taxi draw up, the little scurrying in the hall, the deep thud of the big door closing and the whine of an engine as the taxi went down the drive.

Inez was gone. Not exactly like a thief in the night,
she thought of the uproar in the hall, but not exactly
with banners flying either. But so like Inez! Victoria
knew that she would miss her, miss the little barbs with
which she now coped so well. If Inez had done nothing
else, she had kept Victoria on her toes, and she would
miss the cool, remote elegance which she so much
admired. Victoria sighed and went along to see Abuela.

The two old ladies were sitting by the window.
Sancha, her hands full of grey knitting, was listening
avidly as Abuela read aloud an article describing the
various delights awaiting the tourist in Egypt, nodding
agreement at descriptions of the Sphinx and the
Pyramids. Abuela's husband had been in the Diplomatic
Service and the family and therefore Sancha had lived
for several years in Cairo. When the article was finished,
Abuela folded the paper and rose, leaving Sancha to
concentrate on her knitting.

'Come, *nieta*,' to Victoria, 'we will take a little walk
before tea.'

The patio was sheltered from the wind, although stray
gusts crept into the corners, swirling flower petals and
fallen leaves into little heaps. Abuela shivered and drew
her shawl more closely about her shoulders.

'It grows colder, child. Soon the mountains will have
their covering of snow and winter will be with us again.
There will be skiing and other winter sports on
Candanchu, Carlos will be keeping fires burning
throughout the house with logs from the old apple trees
and we must begin preparations for Christmas—an
English Christmas with a tree, decorations, pudding and
pies. You will have much to do and we shall be very busy.'

'Abuela,' Victoria's voice was hesitant, 'Inez. . . .'

'Yes, I know, *nieta*. Inez has gone,' the old lady
smiled, her still sharp black eyes studying Victoria's
expressive face. 'She has gone to Madrid. It is an

arrangement which I find quite excellent. Her dear friend, Doña Amalia de Soto, is recently widowed and Inez will be a great comfort to her.'

Victoria wrinkled her nose in doubt. Inez a comfort!

'Do not look so,' she was told by an amused Abuela. 'Inez and Amalia were always friends. They are two of a kind, sophisticates. They like the same things, they adore social occasions, they will be very happy. Amalia's husband was elderly, so she has been forced to live a quiet life for many years. Now, after a suitable period of mourning, she will take up her life again. You must remember, Victoria,' the old lady's tone was gently chiding, 'it is not easy for single women of good family to take their place in society, especially if they are still young and attractive. Inez and Amalia will chaperone each other, they will live in Amalia's splendid apartment and go shopping for clothes and otherwise occupy themselves until Amalia is out of mourning and can once more go into society. They will enjoy themselves, I assure you.'

'Inez wasn't happy here, was she?'

'Before you came, child, she was content, shall we say, but it could not last, I knew that. It was inevitable that Rafael would remarry and also that he would not marry Inez. She was hostess and chatelaine here and she did it well, but then she had to make way for you. So, you see, it is much better that she returns to Madrid and takes up a way of life that is more pleasing to her. Now,' her cane tapped the tiles of the patio, 'there is the task of telling Rafael, he could be angry, but I think not. He has known for some time that Inez has been like a fish out of the sea.'

'A fish out of water,' Victoria chuckled. 'Abuela, I do love you! You're so—so sane. He won't be angry about it, surely? I don't see why he should be. Inez is a free agent, so she ought to be able to please herself where she lives. I remember speaking with him about it once and he said only that he would not open up her family house in Madrid. Is it a very large house?'

Abuela was tart. The house was very large, very inconvenient and very ugly. It needed a huge indoor staff to run it properly, at least seven servants and half as many again if one counted the chauffeurs and gardeners. The rooms were lofty and always cold because of marble floors and walls and the furniture. Abuela waved her hands energetically and descriptively. Everything was black, massive and covered with carvings. Abuela's fine old face puckered distastefully. Two maids at least were needed just for dusting and polishing. A house for the *mas ricos hombres*, the very wealthy, or perhaps an hotel. 'It is an idea I will mention to Rafael.'

They went back to the *sala,* where Maria had put the tea tray and a plate of macaroons. Victoria busied herself with the teapot, a heavy silver monstrosity. She thought wistfully of something much smaller and lighter. One could develop muscles like a prizefighter handling this great lump of metal every day! A china one would be nice, she thought, with roses and gold to match the cups. Surreptitiously she inspected the underside of her cup. Royal Albert in a popular design; she would order one.

Her reverie was disturbed by Rafael's deep voice.

'A most felicitous scene—two ladies sipping tea. May we join you?' He gave his wife a smile and she gave him a ghost of a smile back. Windowdressing, she supposed, for the benefit of Juan Martinez who had followed him into the room. Juan was dressed in dandified sportswear, very tight black suede trousers, a white silk shirt with the buttons undone nearly to the waist, thus revealing a smooth, hairless chest decorated with the inevitable gold medallion. Victoria allowed part of her small smile to slide over Juan. Did all Spanish men wear medallions? she wondered. Rafael's was a St Michael who stood stern, his great wings folded and a sword held between his hands. It was usually hidden either by his shirt or the hair on his chest, but one morning she had wakened early and while he still slept, she had examined the bauble. She became aware of Juan's melting eyes roving over her, making her feel uncomfortable.

With hands that trembled slightly, she lifted the teapot, but her husband's strong warm fingers closed over hers. 'From where has come this monstrous thing?' He frowned at it. 'Ah, I remember—my mother used it, did she not, Abuelita? At least she had it used. A servant wielded it for her, I cannot recall her ever lifting it herself. It is too heavy for you, *querida,*' he poured out two more cups of tea and sniffed appreciatively. 'Some good things have come out of England. First, tea and now you, Victoria, but should there not be also a little gossip and, if I recall correctly, according to Oscar Wilde. . . .'

'Cucumber sandwiches,' she finished for him, smiling widely at him for Juan's benefit. 'But that was a long time ago. Life is lived at too great a pace nowadays, especially in the cities, for such niceties. Most women work and it's very hard to stop for tea and cake at four o'clock when you're tied behind a desk until five. In the country, it's a bit different, the pace of life is so much slower. I remember. . . .' She closed her eyes as a faint impression gained strength and blotted out the present. In the spinning darkness behind her eyelids she heard a thin, high-pitched voice fretfully complaining. . . . 'I don't think it's right, sending them to school when anyone with half an eye can see they've got whooping cough. It's not fair on other mothers, is it. . . ?' The whirling darkness cleared and she could see the room, a big, shabby but cosy room with well washed chintz covers on the wide armchairs. The colours of the chintz had faded to a cream with pink and green splodges. On the floor was an old Indian carpet in the same well-worn condition, its central medallion faded to a blur of soft colour. The lace-edged tablecloth had a meticulous darn in one corner, just level with her eyes. A sharp voice said, 'Don't drop it!' and she was looking down with horror at a shattered plate and scattered biscuits. She gasped and opened her eyes; she was back in the *sala* and the other room with its diamond-paned windows and fluttering, ruffled curtains was gone.

Rafael was bending over her and the cold rim of a glass was pressed against her lips. Involuntarily she choked and gulped as raw spirit ran down her throat, making her eyes water. She saw the concern in Rafael's face and the worried frown that knitted little lines in Abuela's forehead. Taking a deep breath, she pushed aside the brandy, staggered to her feet and ran from the room. Halfway up the stairs she stumbled. Hard arms seized her and carried her up to the bedroom and Rafael sat down on a chair, holding her in his arms as if she was a child.

She buried her head in his shoulder and gradually her trembling ceased. She became aware of a strong hand smoothing her hair and the smooth skin of his throat against her cheek. Part in gratitude for the comfort of his arms, she turned her face into his neck and left a soft kiss against his skin. Under her hand she felt his heart beating steadily and she spread her fingers across his chest to feel it more plainly. His breath lifted the short hairs at her temple, she felt his arms tighten about her as the heartbeat under her hand quickened. He gave, what seemed to her to be a cynical laugh.

'Oh no, Victoria! We have a guest. We cannot leave Abuela alone to entertain him, much as I would like to do so. He is staying to dinner, you understand.'

For just a second she felt rage. The conceited, arrogant creature. Just because she had felt a bit grateful to him, he thought that she . . . and then his last remark penetrated.

'I hope he does up his shirt buttons!' She was waspish as he carried her over to the bed, laying her down gently and drawing the covers over her.

'What happened, Victoria?'

'I thought I was going mad.' The strange feeling of being in two places at once swept over her and her voice shook. 'Suddenly I was in another room, different windows, different furniture, a different carpet, and I could hear a woman talking about whooping cough.' She laughed almost hysterically. 'Whooping cough! You don't know what it is, do you? I'd dropped a plate and it had smashed and there were biscuits all over the floor.' She seized his hand and held it tightly. 'Somebody said, Don't drop it, and I did. It smashed to smithereens. There was a darn in the tablecloth, in the corner, I could see it quite plainly.' A thought struck her. 'I must have been quite small, the darn was on a level with my eyes. What's happening, Rafael? Am I remembering?'

'A little, I think.' His voice, deep and thoughtful, was very comforting. 'This is what the doctors said might happen. They also said that you would find it very confusing.'

She gripped his hand hard; suddenly it occurred to her that there might be things which she didn't want to remember. 'Please don't leave me, not just yet. I don't think I want to be alone now.' She felt his long length against her and gratefully turned into his arms. Such a silly idea, she thought, that while she was here nothing could harm her. The steady beat of his heart under her cheek was soothing, very comforting indeed, and her arm tightened over his chest. She felt warm and peaceful and gradually her eyelids drooped. On the edge of sleep, one small thought trickled through her mind. Nobody had told him about Inez yet.

Half an hour later she woke feeling much better. The depression which had rested on her ever since the abortive visit to England was gone completely and she felt incredibly light and happy. The past wasn't going to be such a closed book after all. Perhaps she was going to remember from the beginning. Judging from the height of her eyes in the last episode, she could not have been more than five years old. She let her gaze wander slowly round the darkening room until it came finally to rest on her somnolent husband. No, not somnolent—as she moved her head, his eyes opened.

'So, you wake at last.' His olive-dark face was again a mask of non-expression. 'And we have left Abuela and Juan to entertain each other for long enough, well over half an hour.' He swung his legs off the bed and stood up, surveying his rumpled appearance with a look of distaste. 'I will shower and change and go down. It will soon be dinnertime. Are you hungry?'

Victoria became aware of a very large, very empty hole in her stomach and nodded emphatically.

'Good.' He paused with his hand on his dressing-room door. 'We left rather precipitately, if you remember, so I shall hurry to put Abuela's mind at rest. She will be worrying, and what Juan Martinez will be thinking, I would not care to guess. Also, if we are late for dinner and that might easily happen, then Pilar will become cross and scold us. And you will become bad-tempered with hunger. What it is to be the only man in the family! I am becoming henpecked!'

'Henpecked? You?' Victoria laughed. 'I can't imagine anybody less henpecked than you are. You're ... you're. ... Oh, words fail me!'

'Henpecked,' Rafael reiterated from where he stood, half way through the door. 'A monstrous regiment of women in the house and an argumentative, nagging wife as well. I wonder that I have the strength to survive.' He was laughing as he neatly dodged the pillow she flung at him, catching it and advancing on her, eyes narrowed as he jeered, 'A woman's aim is always uncertain, but me, I never miss.' He lunged forward, trapping her against the bedhead. 'And if I have a nagging wife, I know the cure for that.'

Several seconds elapsed before he reluctantly raised his head and freed her. His nagging wife took a deep breath and let words spill out willy-nilly.

'Bully!' she hurled at him. 'Using your physical superiority to cow and browbeat weak women hardly half your size. You should be ashamed of yourself!'

'That is a new phrase for me, I must remember it. "Cow and browbeat". How do you mean it? I do not beat your brow.'

'Intimidate.' She sat where she was on the bed. She had an idea that she was looking rather rumpled herself and she was too small to be dignified and rumpled at the same time.

When the door closed behind him, she collected fresh underwear and made her way to the bathroom. The mirrors there gave back the reflection of a very far from composed young woman. Her coppery hair, escaping from its neat coil, tumbled untidily about her shoulders, her skirt was creased, her blouse unbuttoned and there was a ladder in her tights. She shuddered. As for her face, there was a wild colour in her cheeks, her nose was shiny and her bottom lip looked slightly swollen. Hastily she removed the offending garments, bundled her hair up under a shower cap and took a leisurely shower. She stood for a long time letting the needle jets play on her back; the cool water was invigorating and she turned her face up to it, closing her eyes with pleasure until she remembered Abuela and Juan.

She pictured them sitting over empty teacups in the *sala*. No—Maria would have removed the tea-tray long before now. Abuela would be gracious and tart by turns. Victoria wondered if, lacking any other company, Juan would make sheep's eyes at Abuela. She gave a muffled little laugh at the mental picture this conjured up. She wouldn't put it past him!

Peering along the hangers in the wardrobe, Victoria found a favourite dress. In fine wool, a sage green

colour, it looked rather mediaeval with its wide sleeves
and low square neck. It suited her, she thought, and
under its long, full skirt, she could wear very high-heeled
sandals so that she would look taller. She brushed and
coaxed her hair into a smooth coil which she wound on
top of her head, securing it with several pins, This would
also increase her height. A large silver-gilt cross on a
thick belcher chain seemed to complement the dress, and
she reviewed the results of her labours in the mirror.
She looked quite nice, not beautiful but pleasant
enough. Some kind fate had given her a smooth creamy
skin, unlike the white one which generally went with red
hair and which freckled abominably.

She certainly looked better than when she had come
from hospital, and she leaned forward to see if she
needed a darker lipstick. The thought of lipstick brought
memories of Inez and her red mouth. Inez! Rafael still
didn't know, unless Abuela had told him. Almost as if
she had conjured him up just by thinking about him, his
dark face appeared behind her in the mirror, and she
turned to him swiftly.

'Inez—she's gone to Madrid, this afternoon before
you came home.'

'Abuela has just told me.' His grey eyes were enigmatic.

'Are you angry?' She looked up at him, searching for
some emotion in the dark, still face above her. 'Shall
you fetch her back?'

'Did I not tell you, only a short while ago, that I
suffer from a surfeit of women?' A smile curved his
mouth. 'No, *señora,* I shall not fetch her back, and I
am not angry. Why should I be? I am thinking now of
how I can rid myself of a few more of my female de-
pendants.' His eyes glinted. 'I could retire Pilar and hire
a chef to replace her; Abuela and Sancha, I could banish
them to a modern apartment in San Sebastian or
Pamplona, and you—no, I think I will keep you.' He

chuckled deep in his throat.

'Will you be serious!' she gasped. 'Retire Pilar, banish Abuela? You're joking, of course!'

'Of course. What chance have I against so many? Pilar would beat me with a rolling pin as she did when I was a boy. As for Abuela and Sancha, Sancha would scold me half to death for causing suffering to her beloved Doña Luisa, and you—you would lash me with your caustic little tongue until I begged for mercy.'

'I can hardly wait for the day!' Victoria eyed him sardonically. 'You begging for mercy, I mean. On your knees, of course, and suitably humble. I doubt I'll live to see the day, but while there's life there's hope.'

They would go one day, he said, changing the subject to the small house in Granada. In the spring when the gardens were beginning to bloom and the Sierras Nevadas were still snow-covered. It was very beautiful then. Just the two of them. There was an expression in his eyes that confused her and set her heart beating erratically. To cover her confusion, she answered him airily.

'Just the two of us? But you won't be able to complain about being henpecked then, will you?'

'That, *querida,* is a debatable point,' he returned swiftly, 'and since Pilar has mountain trout for dinner, we have no time to argue it. However, later perhaps . . .?'

Squabbling amicably, they went downstairs where Juan was waiting for them. Abuela, fresh from Sancha's ministrations, came into the *sala* looking positively regal, rather like a tall, thin Queen Victoria, and her stiff black satin dress rustled importantly.

Before and during dinner, Victoria felt Juan's eyes upon her and each time when she was forced to turn to him, she found herself the recipient of a languishing, sorrowful, almost pitying look. Rafael didn't appear to notice anything untoward, so she contented herself with scowling at Juan every time his hot black eyes travelled over her body.

Escaping upstairs later, she breathed a sigh of relief. She had not emerged entirely unscathed from the ordeal, for at the door, when Juan was making his farewells, she had been forced to submit to having his mouth slobbering over the back of her hand as he wished her goodnight and thanked her, with another hot look, for the hospitality which he had so much enjoyed. She smiled gently at him, although by this time her smile was so rigid that she thought her face would crack.

At nine o'clock the next morning Rafael left for Bilbao. Victoria would have liked to have gone with him, as he was also visiting Santander and he seemed to be in favour of the idea, but Abuela was not well. Victoria bade her husband a staid little farewell and hurried to Abuela's room. She found the old lady propped up in her bed, looking grey and exhausted. Sancha scuttled in with a glass of something which smelled absolutely revolting.

'Whatever is that?' Victoria wrinkled her nose with distaste.

'It is a herbal remedy,' Abuela croaked the words. 'Sancha has a great many recipes for herbal remedies.' Her face registered disgust. 'This is one of the more pleasant ones!'

'It smells lethal—I think you should have the doctor. What you need is a course of antibiotics.' As Victoria spoke, Sancha scuttled out hurriedly. Her goal was the kitchen, where Victoria found her in earnest conversation with Pilar, Maria and Carlos. The amount of opposition Victoria received when she said that she was phoning for the doctor was enormous. Everyone in the household shook woeful heads, as if the very act of sending for a doctor would seal Abuela's doom.

Victoria firmly made her way to the telephone, ordering Sancha, who showed a tendency to cling, to sit with her mistress and perhaps cool her forehead with a cologne-soaked handkerchief.

'Dr Garcia is coming,' she told Abuela a quarter of an hour later,' meanwhile would you like something to drink, something nice?' She frowned at Sancha's latest offering, which stood untouched on the bedside cabinet, and at the old lady's nod, she invaded the kitchen demanding a hot lemon drink with lots of sugar. To this she added a generous portion of whisky, comforting herself that it would be at least two hours before the doctor could arrive and the whisky could not interfere with his treatment after that length of time.

Abuela sipped gratefully and smiled. 'So nice,' she murmured huskily. 'The other remedies they have given me—phaugh! But bronchitis is known as the English disease, is it not? So it is logical that the English should know best how to treat it.'

Sancha, on the other side of the bed, sounded as if she was supplicating every saint in the calendar and was interspersing frantic prayers with ineffectual dabs at Abuela's forehead with a large, cologne-soaked hankie. Victoria frowned at the old maid.

'Doña Luisa needs rest,' and she mercilessly drove Sancha out into the sitting room with instructions to knit or sew or whatever took her fancy in between her fervent prayers to any saints she might have missed the first time round. Looking in from time to time, Victoria found Abuela dozing peacefully. Was it possible that she had overdone the whisky and that Abuela's doze was in fact a drunken stupor?

From the bedside she could hear Sancha's low murmur, and went out to her.

'Did you sleep last night?' she demanded peremptorily, and at the slow shake of the old maid's head, went swiftly back to the kitchen where she prepared a potent hot toddy which she presented to Sancha with two aspirin. Sancha was stubborn; she refused, and Victoria breathed exasperation.

'You are asleep on your feet,' she scolded. 'How can you care for Donã Luisa when you are like this? Take those aspirin, drink that drink and get into bed. I shall need someone to stay with Abuela tonight and you won't be fit, if you don't do as I tell you.'

This terrible thought, together with the equally ter-rifying one that somebody else might take over the care of her dear Donã Luisa, galvanised Sancha into scram-bling into her bed and closing her eyes firmly. Victoria grinned to herself when, less than fifteen minutes later, soft little snores could be heard issuing from Sancha's bedroom.

Dr Garcia was comforting. The bronchitis was a mild attack only. His patient was in good physical condition despite her age, but that age would give cause for con-cern. He wagged an admonishing finger at Victoria, for-bidding any more whisky while his antibiotic tablets were being taken.

'You can expect many more years of useful life.' At these words from a medical man, Abuela sniffed dis-dainfully.

'Go away,' she was tart, 'and don't come back until you've learned better sense!' The old lady annihilated the little doctor with a basilisk stare before closing her eyes. Privately, Victoria thought that Abuela was good for another ten years at least, if will power had anything to do with it.

Juan called in the afternoon, ostensibly to show her his father's new car, a large and businesslike Volvo estate which gleamed a rich forest green in the sunlight. Victoria met him in the hall as she was carrying a jug of lemonade, pure and unadulterated with whisky, to Abuela. Juan had upholstered himself to match the car, in green corduroy velvet. His eyes glowed, his white teeth shone, and she found herself disliking him more than ever.

She declined his offer of a ride, pleading Abuela's illness as an excuse. This gave him the opportunity of offering to provide such comfort and help as she might require by staying by her side for the rest of the afternoon. Her lips twitched as she mentally counted the help available and she sent him home briskly where, she said, she was sure that he would be much more use to his mother than he would be at the Casa or jaunting around the countryside.

Not that the Martinez family were leaving immediately. Señora Martinez, at their last meeting, was deep in fashion and fabric. Olivia was to be introduced into society and the wardrobe full of clothes was but a drop in the ocean to what she would require.

'It will be at least November before we can go,' the Señora had told Victoria. 'There is still so much more that Olivia needs. I have had a dressmaker working full time and it is still not enough.'

Victoria found herself feeling desperately sorry for Olivia, who seemed to be turning into a dressmaker's dummy, but one glance at the young girl's face with its expression of smug satisfaction quickly stifled any feeling of pity she might have had.

CHAPTER EIGHT

THE business of Isabel's leg took longer than had been expected. The visiting orthopaedic consultant did not arrive in Spain as he had planned and a week of silence drove Victoria to the verge of nervous exasperation. The letter which they received from him a week later did little to soothe her.

'He'd no right,' anger and disappointment made her unreasonable, 'having his appendix out instead of coming here as he'd arranged! You'd think that people in his position would have had all those things done well in advance instead of leaving it all until the last moment. In any case, does it have to be this one man? In the whole wide world,' she was becoming heated, 'surely there was somebody else? There are specialists in France, Germany, America. There *must* be somebody who could do it—somebody who's already had their appendix out!'

She ground her teeth in futile rage and was excessively bad company for twenty-four hours. Stormy hazel eyes with green glittering in their depths regarded Rafael across the breakfast table as she bit viciously into a piece of toast.

'If he can't come here,' she demanded belligerently, 'why can't we go there?' She dropped the toast with an expression of distaste. 'Where is he anyway?'

'In London, *amada*.' Rafael's calm didn't help at all, it merely increased her general annoyance. 'We are taking Isabel to him as soon as he has convalesced and is back at his hospital, a matter of a few weeks only. Be reasonable, *querida*. The man did not have appendicitis merely to inconvenience us.'

The storm signals died out of her eyes. 'Why didn't you say so?' she muttered at last, abandoning her attempt to eat the toast. 'Abuela's much better now,

141

quite well, in fact, so we can go any time.' She took a sip of coffee and grimaced. 'What on earth has Pilar done to this coffee, it tastes vile!'

She would go to the kitchen, she decided, and make herself a nice cup of tea She had been drinking too much coffee lately. Halfway to the kitchen, the desire for tea or anything else deserted her, and with a frantic gulp and her hand held tightly across her mouth, she headed at full speed for the small cloakroom off the hall.

It was there that Rafael found her ten minutes later, white, exhausted and, as she could see in the mirror, looking a mess. She pulled herself together and managing a wan, grotesque smile, tried to appear reassuring and hearty.

'I think I may have caught Abuela's 'flu thing.' She closed her eyes to hide tears of vexation and embarrassment that were filling her eyes. Thoughts and ideas ripped through her mind in lightning sequence. Rafael must be worried about Isabel despite his apparent calm. It wasn't right to give him anything more to worry about. Perhaps if she went to bed with some hot lemon and whisky and stayed there for the rest of the day . . .? The thought of lemon and whisky brought about another bout of nausea and she turned back to the handbasin, clinging to the porcelain rim with hands that were cold, damp and trembling.

A week, he'd said. Oh, please let me be over it in a week, she prayed silently, or he'll go without me! Abuela had taken much more than a week to get over her bout, more than a fortnight, but Abuela was an old, old lady and frail. She, Victoria, was young and healthy. Breathe deeply, she told herself. Deep and slow. You'll be all right. It'll pass.

A firm arm came about her, but she pulled herself away.

'It's a bit of a chill, I think.' Sturdily she faced him, her eyes on the third button of his shirt. 'I think I'll go back to bed for an hour or so. When I get up we'll have to start making arrangements. When shall we be leaving next week?'

'I do not think you will be coming, *señora*. You will be better and more comfortable here. I can get a nurse to accompany myself and Isabel.'

Disappointment made her heart go plummeting down and desperation brought her head up. 'But I *want* to go with you. Why shouldn't I? I'm not really ill or anything like that. I'm feeling better already. Just give me a day or two and I'll be fine. Please, Rafael?' She was begging, a thing she had sworn she would never do, she groaned. Whatever was wrong with her, it must be worse than she thought.

His grey eyes surveyed her with deepening amusement and a simply wonderful smile creased his cheek. He wasn't angry, she thought, he was triumphant. He'd brought her to her knees at last. She straightened her back and covered her defiance with a bright smile.

'I'm sorry if I sounded pettish,' she lifted a hand to smooth her hair, 'but I *do* want to come. Give me a minute or so to get a cup of tea and then, while I'm drinking it, you can tell me when we're leaving and how we're travelling. *Not* a ship, Rafael,' she implored, then a thought struck her. 'Isabel will need warmer clothes, it will be colder in London. Shall we buy them here or wait till we get to England?'

His arm barred the door so that she could not pass and now he was openly laughing at her. It was her own fault, she was talking too much, babbling away like a nervous child. His free hand lifted her chin, the thumb caressing the line of her firm little jaw.

'You don't know, do you?' The laughter was even in his voice and she gazed at him with troubled eyes. 'In books,' he continued, 'I believe it is usual for a wife to whisper these little secrets to her husband, but you, my Victoria,' he shook his head ruefully, 'I might have known that you would reverse the normal order. Do you wish me to whisper it to you?'

Victoria blinked momentarily as she absorbed the shock, mentally doing little sums, 'I suppose,' she said defiantly, 'you're trying to tell me I'm pregnant. Well, there's no need for you to be so mealy-mouthed, go about it in such a roundabout way. Whispering secrets!' she sniffed eloquently. 'Why didn't you come right out with it and say, "Victoria, you're in the family way"?'

Rafael was openly laughing at her now. It was a very small cloakroom and in it he seemed bigger than ever. She experienced a wild desire to fling herself against him and let his arms come round her, but that would never do. She glared at him instead. 'Well,' she demanded obstinately, 'what if I am? I don't have to be wrapped in cotton wool, do I? I'm strong and healthy. Other women aren't expected to sit at home twiddling their thumbs just because they're pregnant. Thousands work, they have to, to afford the baby, *and* they go back to work as soon as they can afterwards. In any case, it won't be for ages yet, so I can quite well come to London with you.' She finished triumphantly. 'I won't be left behind!' This afterthought was muttered defiantly only just above her breath.

Rafael quirked an eyebrow at her, obviously puzzled. 'You do not seem overjoyed at the prospect of having a child. You neither look nor sound pleased. You seem to look upon it with resentment, almost, as if it was an inconvenience.'

'I'm in a state of shock,' she explained, adding sarcastically, 'What did you expect me to do, race upstairs and start knitting bootees, or would you prefer me to swoon gracefully at your feet with happiness? I need time to get used to the idea, please. It's all completely new to me and I haven't the least idea what to do. I'll probably make an awful mess of it.' She brightened. 'While we're in London, I'll buy a book about it.'

'*Estupida!* I shall not let you make a mess of it. As for

this London trip, we shall see, although if I leave you behind, I suppose that you will do something foolish. . . . No, on second thoughts, I had better take you with me. Tonight, after dinner, we will discuss plans and arrangements. Where are you going now?' She had finally managed to wriggle under his arm and was hurrying across the hall.

'Upstairs,' she was sardonic, 'to start on the bootees. Sancha is bound to have some wool and needles and a pattern. If I ask her nicely, she'll probably teach me how to knit!' Halfway up the stairs, she stopped and looked down at him still standing at the foot of the stairs and looking at her in a most peculiar way, almost as if she had disappointed him. 'Blue or pink ribbon?' she asked caustically. 'Or doesn't your omniscience stretch that far?'

Once she was in her bedroom, her expression sobered. She examined herself closely in the mirror. She didn't look any different. Almost wearily she sat down at the dressing-table, staring unseeingly at her reflection. Thoughts crowded into her head and her hands twisted together nervously. As if things weren't difficult enough already, without this added complication. Very difficult, she nodded at her reflection gravely. How long had she been in love with Rafael? Days? Weeks? She sighed disgustedly. Not just the ordinary being in love either. She had to go the whole hog. Hers was the 'I'm-down-and-you-can-walk-all-over-me' variety.

'Oh, Victoria,' she breathed, 'you silly starstruck idiot! You don't know how the game is played, and worse than that, you don't know how it's played in his league.' If she knew how Rafael felt, it would be a help, or at least it would if he loved her. But she didn't know how he felt. He seemed very fond of her, but that wasn't being in love with her. She twisted the heavy gold band on her finger. He was a satisfactory husband; she grew warm thinking how satisfactory he was. More than that, *he* seemed to be satisfied, but how long would that last?

The thing to do, she decided, was to carry on as normal, crush down her stupid wild desires to fling her arms around him, hide the wild happiness she felt when he threw her a smile, force herself to remain passive in his arms—and in that, she admitted, she was far from successful. Even if she ever found out how he felt. . . . Perhaps it wouldn't be how she wanted him to feel. She didn't want him to feel bound, obliged. Now her thoughts were getting muddled again!

By dint of strenuous endeavour she had kept their relationship on a light footing over the past few weeks. There had been the usual squabbles, even fights, and all the time she had felt like a skater on thin ice, waiting for the crack which would plunge her into freezing water. When a man is all the things you can dream of, tall, dark, handsome and loaded with money, he doesn't marry a penniless, ordinary creature like you are, she told herself severely. At least he *did* marry you—but not for love! It was her heart that was weeping, she thought as she stared dry-eyed into the mirror.

She wasn't Rafael's sort of woman. His sort of woman was like his first wife, Consuelo, tall, svelte, elegant, an aristocrat to her fingertips, at home in any situation. Victoria unpinned her hair and dragged a brush through it viciously. Not like you! Her reflection stared back at her glumly. Consuelo wouldn't have crashed a car, or if she had, she wouldn't have ended up in hospital with ugly stitches in her head when *he* came visiting. Consuelo would never have precipitated a near-scene in a restaurant or flung pillows and slippers at her husband's head. Consuelo would never have scurried into bed in cotton pyjamas—no! She would have glided across the floor in a silk nightie, dripping with lace.

This attempt at comparisons reduced Victoria to a state of abject misery. She pictured Rafael escorting any number of swanlike, elegant lovelies while she sat at home, lonely, swollen, gross, obscene. There would be a

huge queue of the aforementioned swanlike lovelies,
damn them! And how could he prefer her to them?
Overcome by these gloomy thoughts, she padded over
to the bed and collapsed upon it, tears streaming down
her face. Presently, worn out with emotion, she fell
asleep, to be awakened by Abuela.

'Victoria, child! What is this?' There was concern in
the old lady's voice. 'Rafael has just told me of your news,
so I climbed the stairs and what do I find? Tut-tut,
Victoria, you should not be behaving so. It is not good
for the child.' Her old face and her voice became severe.
'This sort of behaviour makes for a fretful infant. You
will tell me what is wrong. Do you not wish for a child?'

Victoria raised a tear-streaked face from a sopping
pillow and hiccuped mournfully. 'Of course I do, please
believe me, Abuela. Of course I want the baby. But I'm
no beauty now, think what I'll be like in a few months'
time. Rafael won't even want to look at me.' A dazed
look came into her eyes and her face went slack and
white. 'That's what happened before,' she whispered.
'Not to me, to Libby.' She did not appear to see the
consternation on Abuela's face, she was concentrating
on the pictures in her mind. 'I remember it now,' even
her voice was dull and lifeless. 'Libby and I, we roomed
together at university,' pieces of jigsaw were slipping
about in her head and suddenly clicked together. 'Libby
was going to have a baby and she was so happy. I passed
the postman on the stairs, then when I came home at
lunch time, I found her.'

Abuela stiffened and called, 'Rafael!' When he came,
with Sancha labouring at his heels, there was a swift
interchange of Spanish.

Victoria watched dully as Sancha helped the old lady
from the room. Rafael came to sit beside her on the bed
and she did not even turn her head. Her eyes were fixed
on some scene from the past. She felt his hands on her
shoulders, turning her to face him. 'Libby was happy,'

had she said that before? 'Then the postman came and I
passed him on the stairs. I didn't know, I didn't!' her
voice rose hysterically. 'I just went on down and I didn't
come back till lunchtime, till it was nearly too late.'

Rafael shook her. 'What happened, *niña*?' His voice
was sharp, like a teacher wanting, demanding an answer.

Victoria looked at him. If this was remembering, she
didn't want to do it any more. She closed her eyes. 'The
man—he wrote her a letter. He didn't want to see her
again. He said she made him feel sick; and I passed the
postman on the stairs!' Her hands grasped his shirt
front, the fine linen crumpling under her fingers. 'She
tried to kill herself—Libby, who was so happy—and I
didn't come back till lunchtime.'

Strong arms pulled her against a broad chest and she
felt a hand stroking her hair.

'If you must remember something,' he said harshly,
'why must it always be something unpleasant?' She
could feel anger like an electric current flowing from
him. 'Do you think I am a foolish young English boy,
to be seduced by a lissom young body and then find
that body abhorrent because of what I had done? *Basta!*'
The rage cracked in his voice like a whip, stirring her
out of the dull apathy that filled her. 'You are my wife,
are you not? Not a woman I would take to my bed for a
night and forget as quickly.' He shook her again, a little
more severely. 'There are to be no more tears! As Abuela
says, it will make our child fretful and discontented.'

Her apathy vanished in a spurt of rage. 'That's right,'
she exploded, 'you give the orders! No more tears—well,
there won't be, don't worry about that! But when I look
like a whale, you'll smile, damn you, if it kills you, you'll
smile!' A hiccup spoilt the effect of this speech, but she
was quite pleased with it and glared at him, her eyes
very green.

'That is much better, my Victoria.' He smiled down
at her. 'I do not like it when you cease fighting and

dissolve into tears. Do you realise, *niña*, that your little tantrum has taken up most of the morning? Wash your face, tidy your hair and come down to lunch.'

She caught at his hand. 'I wanted so much to remember,' she mumbled, 'but not now, not if it's all bad things. . . .' His finger stilled her mouth as he pushed her gently into the bathroom, where repeated spongings with cold water reduced much of the puffiness around her eyes and a light layer of foundation and a vigorously wielded powder-puff hid the remaining traces of her weeping. By this time she was feeling ravenous and she practically ran downstairs.

'Forgive me, Abuela,' she pleaded as she grasped the thin, blue-veined old hand. 'I upset you, and I shouldn't have done that.'

'Because I am old?' The old voice was tart. 'I have more resilience than you suppose, *nieta*. Not your resilience, though,' she added with a dry smile. 'You are like a rubber ball.'

Lunch was the usual soup and tortillas, but Pilar's chicken soup, creamy, smooth and deliciously spiced, followed by big, fluffy omelettes stuffed with cheese, were just what Victoria needed now that her queasiness had vanished. She found herself enormously hungry and ate with appetite.

'I said before that you were bad-tempered when you were hungry,' Rafael reminded her with a glint in his eyes. 'How are we to manage, Abuelita, while this sickness lasts? There will be tantrums each morning.'

'No, there won't.' Victoria, full of soup, omelettes and satisfaction, was placid. 'It's bad for the baby. Abuela shall teach me self-control.'

After lunch, Abuela's gentle concern and Rafael's stern authority sent her to the bedroom for a siesta. Her objections were pure formality. She was pleasantly full of food and her emotional storm had resulted in a weariness which, although she tried to conceal it showed in her eyes. She kicked off her shoes and dropped on to the bed as she was, pulling the covers over her.

When she woke, chubby little Dr Garcia was sitting by the bed, stethoscope at the ready and a smile all over his plump little olive face.

'Doña Victoria,' he kissed the air one inch above her wrist and pushed a thermometer into her mouth, under her tongue, effectively silencing her while he took her pulse and chatted happily.

He was gratified that he had been called to attend her. His delight at her condition knew no bounds and was exceeded only by his distress that she should have suffered an unpleasant morning. But these little things must not be allowed to upset her.

If Victoria had not been effectively gagged with the thermometer, she would have chorused with him, 'It's bad for the baby!'

'Your memory returns a little, that is good, but that it should be an unpleasant recollection,' he shook his head mournfully, 'that is to be regretted—but one has little choice in these matters.' The thermometer was removed, inspected and shaken down with a practised flip of his hand. 'This girl you knew in London, the affair made a great impression on you?'

Victoria shivered, seeing once again Libby's pallid face and the empty pill bottle on the floor beside the bed.

'Quite so!' Dr Garcia spoke swiftly. 'Therefore you will remember it, while a sweeter, softer memory that did not have the same traumatic effect on you lies dormant in your mind.' Her blood pressure was taken swiftly and competently. 'Now you will rest for the remainder of the day.' Her mouth opened on a protest, but a wave of a plump hand silenced her. 'Your dinner will be brought to you and you will eat it. Then you will take these two small tablets,' he laid two pills carefully in a small dish on the bedside table, 'and then you will sleep.'

'I will?'

'Yes,' the little dumpling of a man spoke with a plump little authority, 'and when you wake tomorrow morning, your troubles will be as mist in the sunlight—vanished! You will see things again properly, in proportion, and you will realise how small are the woes that beset you. You have so much, Doña Victoria—a beautiful home, a loving husband, and later there will be your child.' He gathered up his impedimenta and tucked it firmly in his bag. 'See, here is the *moza* with your tea. Such comfort! *Adios,* Doña Victoria, we shall meet next month when I shall call on you again.' Smiling benignly, he closed his bag with a snap and trotted out, leaving Maria who plumped up pillows, stuffing them behind Victoria until she was propped upright.

There were two cups and saucers on the tray and within a few moments Rafael came to join her. She went pink as his eyes roved over her, conscious of untidy hair and rumpled attire. She wished vainly that she had bothered to undress before flopping on the bed as she had done.

'Yes, *querida*, you look better. Admit now that the siesta is a very pleasant way of life. One rises refreshed to face the evening.'

'You don't take one,' she argued.

'If by that you mean that I do not sleep, you are correct, but I do relax.' He deftly poured tea and handed her the cup and saucer. 'In the summer, the siesta is most necessary, especially when it is very hot. One stays peaceful behind drawn blinds and cool behind closed shutters. Children allowed to play in such heat in the afternoons become tired and fretful, too tired to eat their meals, too fretful for sleep. No, *querida*, perhaps you do not need this little rest in England, but in Spain we do.'

Victoria drank her tea thirstily and passed her cup for refilling. The tea revived her and this combined with the beneficial results of an hour's rest had restored her to the reasonable human being she normally was. She stole a sideways glance at Rafael, sitting there at his ease, and a delightful little bubble of happiness swam up inside her and seemed to burst in her throat, making her want to laugh out loud.

Her eyes flicked over his black head, just a little silvered at the temples, his dark face, the strong column of his throat, the long slender hands that were so sensitive. Love was a strange thing, she mused. It had crept up on her silently and occupied her before she was even aware of it. One day she had questioned it and the next it was a blinding certainty and nothing else mattered. Maybe she wouldn't have all the trimmings, maybe she would never make the bells ring for him, but that didn't matter any more.

He broke in on her musings. 'The play of expression across your face is fascinating, *pequeña*. First there is doubt, then a small determination, then a soft secret happiness. You have accepted the idea of the child, you are happy about it?'

Victoria turned wide hazel eyes on him and a smile curved her mouth. 'Yes, I've accepted it, I've accepted everything.' The last few words she breathed to herself. 'I may come with you to England, though, mayn't I? I'll promise to do everything you say, I won't overtire myself, I won't argue. I'll do everything you say. I'll do just as I should.'

The look of patent disbelief on her husband's face was not conducive to sweetness and light, in fact it caused her to have second thoughts on the promises she had just made. If he wasn't going to believe her then she might just as well . . . she caught herself quickly. Wasn't she going to be sensible from now on? Not precipitate quarrels! As she came to this decision, she heard herself say indignantly,

'If you're going to look like that, it's no good, is it?'

'How am I looking, *querida*?'

'As if you don't believe a word I say, as if you don't trust me.'

He burst into rare laughter, laughter of pure amusement. 'Oh yes, *querida*, I believe you and I trust you also. I know that you will do everything I say, you can be sure of that! Now drink your second cup of tea and rest yourself.'

Over the rim of her cup she explained Dr Garcia's instructions. 'It was just like listening to the Ten Commandments, only instead of all those "Thou shalt nots" there were about a dozen "You wills" and most of them were quite ridiculous. I've no intention of staying in bed. I'll be down to dinner as usual. I'll have a bath and dress and come downstairs. It's ridiculous having Maria trail up and down with trays and things, and I loathe eating in bed.'

Deftly Rafael removed the cup from her fingers and set it beside his own on the tray, before he took her small, determined chin in his fingers. He lowered his dark head and kissed her mouth, and the sweetness of it brought the tears to her eyes. She slid her arms up over his shoulders, her fingers moving in the crisp, short hair at the back of his head. Several seconds passed in utter silence before he lifted his head and grasped her shoulders in a far from gentle hold. Reluctantly Victoria descended from Cloud Nine and opened her eyes.

'No, Victoria, I am not to be seduced so,' he told her firmly. 'I will send Maria to you and you may certainly take a bath, it will refresh you, but afterwards you will return to bed as the doctor instructed and stay there for the rest of the day. Tomorrow, we will see. Besides, I believe that young Martinez is in the *sala* with Abuela at this very moment. I do not think that you like that young man, and if you come down to dinner, he will beg an invitation and we will not see him go before midnight.' He shook his head at her rebellious expression, his mouth firm. 'Your dinner will be brought to

you here and when you have eaten it, I will come and
we will talk a little about the trip to London.'

His obedient wife glared at him in pure frustration.
'You're nothing but a tyrant,' she grumbled.

He nodded serenely and went away to shower and
change. The only thing that pleased Victoria was that
she would avoid Juan. Rafael was quite right in saying
that she did not like him; she disliked him very much.
He made her angry and embarrassed with his patting
hands, his hot black eyes and his full red mouth that
slobbered over her hands.

Victoria was surprised to find how wobbly she felt
when she went to the bathroom and even more surprised
when, instead of Maria, Pilar came. The gargantuan
cook was beaming all over her face and every inch of
her massive form exuded delight and satisfaction.

'*Encinta*—pregnant!' Her stentorian tones, although
respectfully muted, rang round the bathroom as Victoria
found herself lifted from the bath by a pair of arms
which would have put a navvy to shame. 'We all have
great joy.' This was in Spanish but spoken very slowly
so that Victoria could understand. She was enveloped in
a huge bath towel and firmly rubbed dry while Pilar
continued to be delighted. She prophesied not one but
many children, all beautiful. The silk pyjamas which
Victoria had collected on the way to the bathroom were
dismissed with scorn.

'Such garments are only for *niños* and men. The
Señora is a woman and should dress like one, even in
bed—especially in bed, otherwise how should there be
babies?' Pilar's laugh boomed and echoed from the
bathroom tiles. 'What man wishes to take to his bed a
niño, a boy? Where would be the pleasure in that?' Still
talking at full volume and in the middle register, Pilar
went away to root through drawers, returning with a
nightdress in apple green silk into which she swiftly
inserted her mistress.

Pilar stood back and breathed a huge sigh of admiration. 'The Señor will be enchanted,' she informed Victoria as she brushed and braided the long copper hair and tied the ends of the plaits with green ribbon before pushing her into bed.

Pilar's unaffected delight and earthy comments woke an instant response. Victoria, on the edge of laughter, allowed herself to be swept back into bed and tucked up like a child. Lace-edged pillows were stuffed behind her and a lacy bedjacket in fine wool was brought to cover her shoulders.

'From Doña Luisa—very beautiful,' Pilar explained as Victoria fingered the cobwebby texture.

Left alone, Victoria felt like a worm. Everybody was being so kind, so genuinely concerned, so happy for her, and she suspected that she did not deserve it. She had behaved like a perfect pest over lots of things. The trip to England, for instance, not the one coming but the abortive one in search of her memory. For all the trouble and inconvenience it had caused, what had she got from it but a dose of seasickness? It was about time, she decided, that she grew up. Meanwhile, she was wallowing in comfort and attention.

Abuela came tapping across the room at six o'clock to take a seat by the bed and survey her grandson's wife. Her long black skirts swished to the tap of her cane and her silver hair glinted through the fine lace of her mantilla. Victoria impulsively kissed the hand extended to her, a very elegant hand in a black lace mitten. She thanked the old lady for the bedjacket, inwardly marvelling that Abuela should be so kind and thoughtful to somebody who had turned the house upside down with tantrums.

'*Es nada,*' it's nothing, was the old lady's brisk retort. 'What use have I for such things at my age? Have I not a chest full of such things, shawls and wraps without number, and is not Sancha continually adding to them?'

'But it is beautiful.' Victoria tenderly stroked the fine wool and the silk floss trimming. 'I've been a pest, haven't I?' she muttered apologetically. 'Having hysterics and setting the whole house by the ears.'

Abuela nodded serenely. 'But you will no longer behave so, I am sure. You are an intelligent girl and your disposition is kind and thoughtful. So now you will busy yourself with preparations for your child and your mind will be content. You will cease to behave like a——' she hesitated, 'I do not think we have a suitable phrase in Spanish. In French, I would say, a *garçon manqué*. You would call it a tomboy?'

The lace-mittened hand waved with authority. 'You will discard your dreadful trousers, which garments are fit only for boys and men, and dispose yourself to be a woman and a mother. You will find great satisfaction in this; so there must be no more storms and tears.'

Under the stern gaze from the still beautiful dark eyes, Victoria found herself flushing. Abuela laughed gently. 'Yes, child, I know it has been difficult. Without memories you must have felt like a rootless plant. But they return now, do they not? In any case, it is the future that is important to you now. When you are as old as I am, then you can turn to memories. Now that you are young, you must look forward.' There was a gentle pat on her hand, the gentle touch of a withered cheek against her own, and Abuela smiled down at her. 'Sancha has already started the knitting of small garments, and for this I must thank you. I have grown very tired of seeing those grey socks for ever on her needles!'

Maria bustled in promptly at eight o'clock with an enormous tray. There was a cup of bouillon, she demonstrated, lifting covers to display the contents of dishes. Here was a portion of chicken poached in wine with a good cream sauce, here a small green salad, a caramel cream and a glass of wine. Of coffee there would be none, it did not induce a good night's sleep, but

should the Señora desire it, she would receive a glass of
hot milk which would be better for the child—and Maria
nodded her seventeen-year-old head with all the wisdom
of a grandmother.

Victoria choked on a smile of amusement as Maria
listed the nourishing and sustaining qualities of the
various dishes before whispering that her mother
intended to inspect the tray on its return to the kitchen,
apparently to satisfy herself that the Señora was not
likely to die of starvation during the night.

'It's such a family affair,' she told Rafael after dinner
as he sat lazily by the side of the bed, his long limbs
disposed in a tall-backed chair. A soft light from the
bedside lamp illuminated his face. He looked, she
thought, rather like an El Greco painting, brought up
to date. El Greco would have given him a little pointed
beard to emphasise the long ascetic features, but otherwise the high forehead, hooded eyes and aquiline nose
fitted very well. As did his hands, long and slender
without being in the least effeminate. If he had been a
painting, one of those hands would have been resting
on the hilt of a sword, while the other fiddled with an
ornament about his neck. On the whole, Victoria mused,
she preferred him holding the long cigarette.

His calm deep voice penetrated her musings just as
she had clothed him in doublet and hose with a starchy
white ruff about his neck. She dragged herself back
quickly to the present.

'But of course, did you think they would have no
interest? Pilar, Carlos, Maria, even little Carlota—they
are our people, they consider this house as much theirs
as ours. They see us as part of their family, to be cared
for and cared about as they would their own relatives.
Anything we do is of great interest to them, they feel
they are part of it. Do you understand this attitude? It
is not all one way. We in our turn are expected to take a
more than passing interest in them and their lives.'

Almost absentmindedly, he had taken one of her plaits in his hand and was carefully unbraiding it, winding the tresses around his fingers. 'When Maria marries, it is I who will give away the bride, not Carlos who is her father, and it is you who will provide the wedding dress, not Pilar.' He smiled at her through a cloud of cigarette smoke. 'You will possibly have to go with Pilar to inspect Tomás's farmhouse to see that it is fit for Maria to live in, and,' he gave a rather sardonic laugh, 'you will possibly have to console the mother of Tomás and convince her that she does not lose a son when she gains a daughter. I do not envy you your task, *esposa mia*, that one is a doting *mama* who considers that nobody is good enough for her son and she is going to fight tooth and nail to keep him for herself. She will lose, of course,' he mused, a hint of mockery curving his mouth. 'Tomás is young and Maria is very pretty, but there will undoubtedly be fireworks before the wedding day.'

Victòria swallowed her tablets and drank her hot milk. 'It sounds very feudal.' The milk made her feel warm and cosy inside. It didn't go with apple green silk nighties, though. Children in flannelette pyjamas drank hot milk, not sophisticated women in silk. 'Very oldfashioned.' The words came out slightly blurred—the effect of Dr Garcia's knock-out drops, she thought hazily, and tried to say so. 'Very effective,' she managed before her eyes closed.

She didn't hear Rafael leave the bedroom, nor did she stir when he returned two hours later. He showered and slid into bed beside her, gathering her close, her head on his shoulder.

Drowsily, she half opened her eyes and smiled at him. She mumbled something as she snuggled against him, her eyes closing almost immediately so that she missed his rueful smile, nor did she feel the light kiss he dropped on her hair.

CHAPTER NINE

DESPITE the onset of winter, the journey to London was delightful. They went leisurely by car with Rafael driving and Victoria either sitting by him or playing with Isabel in the back seat. Isabel chattered happily. She had brought with her a favourite doll, a Teddy bear and a large notebook, together with some felt-tipped pens. Rafael had planned the journey well, so that each afternoon they drew up at the hotel or auberge where they were to spend the night, all in good time for Isabel to see the various points of interest and to look in shops with Victoria, comparing prices and quality avidly.

Isabel noted everything down in her book—the towns through which they passed, the rivers they crossed, the meals they ate en route and the names of the hotels at which they stayed. Each evening, colourful postcards were posted to Abuela, Sancha, Carlos and Pilar, Sister Teresa at the convent and to innumerable school friends.

After they left Tours, the weather steadily worsened and Victoria, a sinking sensation in her stomach, found herself regarding the cross-channel ferry at Calais through a grey curtain of rain. Silently she prayed for a quiet crossing, although outwardly subscribing to Isabel's desire to see waves, as huge as possible.

'Nothing would please me more,' she assured the little girl. 'I would like to see waves as high as the ship, but it would make it a very dull voyage. We should have to stay in the cabin all the way and that would be a pity. We should miss seeing the other ships in the Channel and we might not notice the white cliffs of Dover.'

Isabel was a reasonable child and readily reduced the

159

size of the waves she required. 'It's very stuffy in the cabin,' she said agreeably, 'and there's only that one small round window and I can't see through it. Shall we see other ships? Will they be bigger than this one?'

'If we see an oceangoing liner or an oil tanker,' Victoria promised, 'it will be much bigger than this.'

Much to her surprise, Victoria felt no qualms of sea-sickness at all. She enjoyed the crossing immensely and felt that it was partly due to Isabel's enthusiasm. They walked the decks and watched the water slip past, they went ferreting for souvenirs in the duty-free shops and drank fizzy lemonade at a table in the lounge. Isabel bought ballpoint pens with the name of the ship on the plastic barrels as gifts for her school friends.

It was still raining at Dover which, in a way, compensated Isabel for the white cliffs of Dover not being so very white—in fact, the rain made her very happy.

'Sister Teresa told us that in England there is always very much rain, more rain than anywhere else, and that people in England must always wear mackintoshes and carry umbrellas when they go out. Sister Teresa says that there is more rain here than in Santander, and there it is very wet.'

Rafael caught the end part of this conversation as they went down to the car deck. 'Sister Teresa would seem to be an authority on most subjects,' he smiled down at his small daughter as she struggled with a large plastic carrier bag which contained most of her treasures. He hoisted her on to his shoulder at the top of the steps and carried her the rest of the way to the car.

Off the ship, Rafael drove sedately on the London road, and Isabel commented on the number of mackintoshes and umbrellas with satisfaction.

'Sister Teresa was quite right, Papa. Nearly everybody has an umbrella. I expect that I shall need one also.'

'Sister Teresa would seem to be infallible,' he murmured.

Unfortunately the rain had stopped when they at last reached London, and only the promise of a shiny mackintosh and her very own private umbrella reconciled Isabel to dry streets, a clear though rather grey sky and gutters that were not full of rushing water.

As they were not due to see the specialist for several days, the intervening time was to be spent in sightseeing. Isabel did not think very much of the Tower of London, there were bigger and better castles in Spain. Windsor Castle was more to her taste. It looked more like a castle should look, and if somebody in authority would only have taken the Yeomen Warders and the ravens down to Windsor, Isabel would have been completely happy.

Nelson's Column held no joy for her either, although she thought the lions at the base were quite pleasant. She would have preferred Nelson to have been farther down where she could see him properly. Buckingham Palace did not disappoint her, but a glimpse of the Queen did. The Queen was not wearing a crown or even a coronet, but a hat like any other lady, and she was seated not in a beautiful coach or carriage and drawn by beautiful horses but in an automobile—a very beautiful automobile, but not to be compared with the coach of which she had seen pictures.

Isabela's joy and delight were the double-decker buses. She watched them with fascination, for a while quite convinced that they were going to fall over when they went around corners, and she was hugely relieved when they did no such thing. She liked best of all to ride in them, at first on the lower deck and then as her confidence in their stability increased, upstairs, seated as near to the front as possible with her nose pressed to the glass of the window, watching people on the pavements below her. It was superb when it rained because she then had an uninterrupted view of umbrella tops.

They fed the ducks in Regent's Park and the swans along the Thames. Isabel watched with awed wonder the opening of Tower Bridge to let a ship pass through. She jigged happily to the Changing of the Guard at St James's Palace and stared with patent disbelief at the porters in the new Covent Garden Market with their piles of baskets on their heads, and she spent a whole afternoon in the Planetarium.

At the end of three days of behaving like tourists, Victoria collapsed on her bed in the hotel with a groan of complete and utter weariness. Isabel was tucked up in her own bed in an adjoining room, bathed, fed and sleeping the sleep of a contented child.

Tomorrow she would rise refreshed and full of vigour, ready to plunge on to yet another of her beloved double-decker buses. Victoria, with aching feet and a severe headache, groaned again. There was so much more! The British Museum, Madame Tussaud's, Whipsnade, Hampton Court Palace and the Maze, Kew Gardens, Petticoat Lane, the Post Office Tower—the list was endless. Isabela had every item down in her notebook with little ticks against those that had been visited, and so far there seemed to be more empty spaces than ticks!

Rafael regarded his supine wife with a hard grey gaze.

'Tomorrow,' he declared, 'is a day of rest.'

'Tomorrow,' his wife contradicted, 'is Sunday. Petticoat Lane in the morning and the Zoo in the afternoon. Don't you remember?'

'I remember very well, and to Petticoat Lane Isabel shall go with me, but you will rest. Perhaps after lunch and if you are less tired, I will permit you to accompany us to the Zoo.'

'You will permit!' The light of battle dawned in her eyes, but before she could speak, he continued smoothly,

'Do you tell me then, *querida,* that your promises mean nothing? You recall them? That you would not tire yourself, that you would not argue with me, that you would do as I said. These were, then, merely empty words. Is that what you mean?'

Reluctantly, she shook her head and swung her legs off the bed to sit upright. 'I'm not tired,' she protested, 'well, not *very* tired. I admit that it has been a bit hectic, but I've enjoyed every moment of it, and tomorrow is the last real day, isn't it? On Monday, Isabel sees the specialist. One more day, Rafael, please! I don't want to spoil anything for Isabel. Then I'll lie in bed every day until noon if you like.'

'More promises?' He tilted her face up, his thumb smoothing her cheekbone. 'No, *querida*. Your concern for Isabel makes me very happy, but what of our child—your child? You could so easily exhaust yourself and do some damage, even lose the baby. As I said, the Zoo, if you are rested, but no Petticoat Lane; and do not argue with me, my mind is made up.'

'Brute!' answered his wife amiably, but later, as she luxuriated in a hot foam bath, she found that her defiance was not as great as her relief. The prospect of a lovely, lazy Sunday morning was very inviting. Thinking about it, Victoria was quite surprised to find that, as far as she was concerned, the sooner that they returned to the Casa, the better she would be pleased.

She no longer felt at home here in England, she had become too used to the slower pace of life in Navarre. The constant roar of London traffic assaulted her ears and the hurrying crowds of people, all of them anonymous and uninterested, made her feel like a stranger in her own country. She missed the daily consultations with Pilar, even though they were mainly carried out in sign language with the occasional word thrown in when she could remember the right one. She had so much to tell Abuela and Carlos and even Sancha's querulous complaints, although they were often infuriating, would have been very welcome in her ears at this moment.

Victoria gave a rueful smile to herself. It would seem

that she had become more Spanish than English, and it was very nice to have her own little sphere to manage, her own house to retreat into and to cast everything else on to Rafael's shoulders.

The cooling bathwater brought these pleasant but unprofitable thoughts to an end, but not before she had decided that Rafael had very nice shoulders.

The visit to the hospital on Monday had Victoria jittering even before they left the hotel. Not so Isabel; Isabel sparkled at Mr Clarke Stevens, the consultant, who spoke in jerky phrases, like a telegram; and she went off happily to have X-rays taken. She had been in many hospitals before, she explained to Victoria, and they were all the same, so there was no need for anybody to accompany her except the charming nurse who wore such a charming cap. It was not long and flowing as it was in many Spanish hospitals, but small with starched frills and strings which tied under the nurse's chin in a further frilly bow. Victoria found herself left with Rafael and silently agonised in a quite pleasant waiting room which was attached to the consultant's office.

What if nothing could be done? The hands of the clock on the wall moved on at a snail's pace, minute by dragging minute. Sometimes when she looked, they seemed not to have moved at all. She felt a cold dampness on her forehead and moving swiftly, she crossed to the window, standing there to look out upon the grassy square below her. It wasn't an entrancing view, but it was better than sitting in the hard-backed chair and just waiting.

The pocket handkerchief of green was surrounded by a high wall of rosy bricks and bisected by a narrow tarmac path. After she had been watching it for a few minutes, a group of nurses crossed the green, white-capped, their scarlet-lined capes fluttering in the brisk breeze. To Victoria, it was all a blur of green, white, scarlet and navy blue under the pale sunlight. Her mind was on the future, Isabel's future, and there was no room in it for anything else.

Rafael came to stand beside her and she turned a white anxious face to him.

'Supposing they can't . . .?' Her voice was hoarse and stumbling and her eyes were dark pools with only hazel flecks in them. She felt his arm about her, close, comforting, and she turned her face into his chest. He gave her a little shake.

'If they can do nothing, then that is how it must be, Victoria,' his voice was sombre. 'You must be sensible. Have you ever seen Isabel anything but happy? Have you ever heard her complain?'

'No,' she gulped, 'but that doesn't make it any better!'

'Yes, it does.' His voice was firm, almost scolding. 'Isabel is, I think more grown up than you are. She accepts, you fight. There are two sides to the moon, a dark side and a bright side, and you cannot have one without the other. Isabel knows this and accepts it. She knows that she has much that others might envy. She does not weep for herself and she would not wish you to weep for her. If she must remain as she is, it will not make her less happy. If something can be done, she will simply be more happy and if not now, perhaps later. Each year brings new techniques. Ah!' He released her and turned to the door. 'Someone is bringing some tea. Come, *mi mujer*, have a cup of your so British beverage. In moments of crisis, I understand the British seek their courage, not in a bottle but in a teapot. I have often wondered why you as a nation are so different from the rest of the continentals, and I think that I now know. It is your tea!'

Victoria gave him a watery grin. The tea was hot, sweet and comforting. She was on her second cup when the consultant returned.

'Tea—good!' Mr Clarke Stevens accepted the cup she

handed him, loaded it with sugar and stirred it thoughtfully while he spoke in the same brief jerks as he had
done previously. 'Nice little girl. Speaks good English
too—surprising! Always limp, you know. Always have
a weakness there. Want her to see a friend of mine—
Dutch fellow, very clever. Possible to get rid of that
brace, ugly-looking thing.'

Victoria let out the breath she had been holding with
an audible gasp and turned brimming hazel eyes upon a
horrified Mr Clarke Stevens who had tagged her as one
of those 'volatile continental types' and was secretly
afraid that she might kiss his cheek or, worse still, both
cheeks. He went rather red in the face and hurriedly put
the width of the table between them. 'Not this year,
though. Van Decker's in America. Make arrangements
when he's back. Interesting, very interesting.'

With a brief mutter of apology, Victoria got herself
out of the room, leaving Rafael to cope with the consultant and cover such mundane matters as when and
where. Out in the corridor, she leant her clammy forehead against the cold plaster of the walls and wept with
relief and happiness. By the time that Isabel and her
frilly nurse returned, Victoria had mopped her eyes,
blown her nose and was able to turn a smiling face to
the world.

The three of them had dinner that night together in
the hotel dining room, Isabel, as a treat, being allowed
to stay up late. She sat at the table sedately, beaming at
Victoria across the little flower arrangement on the
centre of the table.

'Next year, and that is only two months away now, I
will be going to Amsterdam, to see the Dutch doctor.
Your English doctor says that he is a wizard and that
he can fix my leg so that I do not have to wear this
brace any more. The English doctor says that it is very
ugly. Is it not wonderful!' Isabel spooned iced pudding
into her mouth and heaved a huge sigh of content.

'I shall only have a very little limp, which is nothing, and I shall be able to ride my pony and perhaps a bicycle when I come home. And then,' her black eyes sparkled, 'there will be a little baby and I shall be able to come home every weekend. Life is going to be *so* exciting!'

Rafael's grey eyes looked 'I told you so' at Victoria, who coloured slightly and smiled back. There was no time for any adult conversation, words tripped from Isabel's tongue in a seemingly never-ending flow.

'Tomorrow Papa is taking us to Hampton Court and we will find our way to the very centre of the Maze and I shall take many snapshots with my camera. Then, on Wednesday, Papa is taking us home. There will be the ship and the long journey through France.' Isabel's eyes sparkled with enthusiasm and her small face radiated happiness under the bouncing black curls.

As she was being tucked up in bed, she explained to Victoria, 'It is all as Papa said it would be, and Sister Teresa must have prayed very hard to make it all come right—to make the doctor such a nice man and for the baby to be coming.' Isabel covered Victoria's face with a great many moist kisses and announced that she was the happiest girl in the world before her eyes closed and sleep overtook her.

Returning to the dining-room, Victoria found that a small orchestra was now playing and that several couples were dancing on the pocket-handkerchief-sized area left clear of tables. Rafael rose and drew her on to the dance floor. There wasn't much room for dancing, but it was very nice to be there in the circle of his arms, swaying gently to and fro to the dreamy music. More couples joined those already on the floor and she moved closer to him, closing her eyes and drifting dreamily into a fantasy world where he loved her as much as she loved him. The music ceased and she reluctantly unplastered herself from him to return to their table and to the real

world where he did not, unfortunately, love her as much
as that. But he did love her a little, in his own way, she
was sure of that, and it would have to be enough. She
would make it enough. She would, as he had said, concentrate on the bright side of her own particular moon
and whenever possible ignore the dark part.

Rafael was smiling down at her when the waiter came
hurrying with champagne in an ice bucket.

'A little celebration.' There was pleasure and satisfaction in his voice.

'Isabel . . . I'm so glad!'

'Not only Isabel.' His eyes travelled over her still
slender body. 'We have another cause for celebration,
not apparent as yet,' he continued smoothly, 'but worthy
of celebration, don't you agree, *mi esposa*?'

Victoria felt hot colour in her cheeks, but she kept
her voice prosaic. It cost her some little effort, but she
congratulated herself on achieving a creditable facade
of normality.

'Oh yes, definitely worthy of celebration.' She took a
heady draught of champagne and felt the bubbles tickle
the roof of her mouth. 'I think I've been very clever,
don't you?'

He refilled her glass. 'Clever? No, that is not the correct word, *querida*. I can think of several others which
are much more apt. However, finish your champagne
and we will have one more dance, then it is your bedtime. Tomorrow, as Isabel took care to remind us, we
go to Hampton Court.'

She nodded. 'I'm glad about that too. Isabel was so
looking forward to it, and to the Maze. You know,
Rafael,' she leaned forward, 'I've thought about what
you said at the hospital and you're quite right. The good
news just makes her happier. If it hadn't been good, if it
had been bad, it wouldn't have been so bad after all.
I'm not making much sense, am I?' Ruefully she smiled
at him. 'But that's your fault.'

'My fault?' A black eyebrow raised in an arrogant query.

'Your fault, definitely. I'm not used to champagne and I've had two glasses of the stuff. It's very efficacious at removing inhibitions and muddling up my ideas.' She half rose from her chair, but his hand captured her arm and drew her back.

'We will order another bottle at once,' he decreed. 'My Victoria with all her ideas muddled and her inhibitions thrown to the winds! This I must see.'

Laughing at him, she shook her head. 'No, Rafael. We'll do as you first said. One more dance and then to bed. No more of that,' she gestured at the empty bottle. 'It might not be good for the baby, he might grow up to be a wine-bibber. I really must get a book about it,' she murmured, 'or have deep consultations with Pilar and Abuela. They ought to know.'

Lying back against her pillows, she watched Rafael as he made ready for bed. He eyed the twin beds with an arrogant disgust.

'I shall be more than happy to be back home soon,' he told her. 'This separate existence,' he waved his hands at the twin beds, 'it is abhorrent to me.'

Perhaps it was the champagne, still sparkling in her blood, that made her giggle. 'The trouble with continentals is their inherent inability to overcome minor obstacles,' she finished the sentence with a yelp as he began to demonstrate that there was one continental at least to whom obstacles, minor or major, were no deterrent at all.

Isabel glowed all the way across the Channel and right through France. Beside her on the back seat of the car was a large and bulging carrier bag decorated with colourful Union Jacks and containing an exciting selection of small gifts for her school friends, teachers, Abuela and the rest of the household. Whenever the journey became boring, she tipped out the contents of the bag on to the seat and went over each neatly wrapped parcel, naming its recipient and counting carefully each time to ensure that not one precious package had been lost.

After the hustle and bustle of London, Victoria was glad to relax. She was going home. Within two short days she would be safely back in the Casa. Rafael had been quite right in a way; it had been a tiring time. She had enjoyed every moment of it, but now she was content to sit and watch his long slender hands on the wheel and, now and then, to glance at his face when she thought he wasn't looking.

CHAPTER TEN

THE letter lay on Victoria's lap, a thick, cream-laid envelope stuffed with matching sheets of paper. 'From the Señor Martinez,' was what the man had said when he delivered it into her hands. She had been on her way down to the *sala* when Carlos had opened the door. The messenger had looked half drowned—and no wonder!

Heavy rain driven by gale force winds was a slanting, solid sheet of water outside the door. It was hurled against the walls and it battered savagely at the windowpanes. Now and then a crash could be heard as a heavy flower tub was plucked from its place by the wind and sent hurtling on to the tiles of the patio. The mule which the man had been riding through the storm stood, its back to the wind, its head down, ears flopping miserably.

'Tell him to get it to the stables!' Victoria had to shout to make herself heard over the banshee howling of the wind. Carlos shook his head and shrugged.

'For the mule, nothing can be done, *señora*. It will stand there and the water will pour over it and run off as it is doing now. It will come to no harm. The messenger, however, he can be taken to the kitchen and dried. I will attend to it.' Carlos and the man struggled with the heavy door to shut it against the screaming wind and at last managed to shut it. Carlos turned back to Victoria. 'There is nothing that you can do, *señora*, and it is cold here in the hall. You should go into the *sala* where it is warm and read your letter. Pilar will attend to this unfortunate fellow. Go into the *sala*, please, *señora*.'

Carlos looked so pleading that Victoria smiled wryly.

There was a conspiracy among all of them, Carlos, Pilar, Maria, even little Carlota, to keep her away from anything that might be in the least unpleasant or had anything to do with work. She trotted off to the *sala*, her mind working at top speed trying to guess the contents of the letter before she opened it. The direction was quite plain, Señora Alvarez; it was definitely for her.

She sat on the couch which Carlos had drawn up before the fire and turned the letter over between her fingers and then, almost with reluctance, she opened it. On the last of the thick sheets of notepaper the signature 'Juan' leapt out at her—a scrawled, immature signature. Victoria sniffed her displeasure. She was now cross. Juan should have thought before he sent a man ten miles on a mule in this weather! She was sorry for the man and even sorrier for the mule. With a small sigh of despair at such thoughtlessness, she started to read her letter, interrupting her perusal very often to think about the dripping messenger and his even wetter steed.

To send a man on a mule in this weather was an act of folly and complete disregard for others. She had always thought that Juan was stupid, and this latest piece of nonsense merely confirmed her in her opinion. The gale hurled more rain against the windows and involuntarily she shivered, although the room was warm enough.

Abuela and Sancha were together in their sitting-room. 'Storms upset Sancha,' Abuela had been sympathetic. 'We shall sit there together and I shall read to her. You are not nervous, Victoria?' With a shake of her head, Victoria put Abuela's mind at rest and the old lady had gone off to her own apartments which fortunately were in a part of the house sheltered from the prevailing wind.

It was nearly five o'clock. Victoria glanced at her watch and compared it with the brass carriage clock on the mantelshelf. Rafael should be home soon, this weather wouldn't stop him. She went back to the letter, smoothing out the paper and looking at the undisciplined scrawl with distaste, her mind going back to Rafael. If a man on a mule could come from the Martinez house then Rafael could come from San Sebastian in a Mercedes. It would take him a little longer than it usually did, that was why he was late.

Again, with reluctance, she let her eyes skim the letter, frowning as she tried to decipher it. It was just as well, she thought, that Juan was a member of the family and was going to be made a junior partner in the business because, as an ordinary clerk, he would not have lasted five minutes, if this misspelled, raggedly written effusion was an example of his ability. Even allowing for the fact that he had written the letter in English which he spoke well enough, it was a very poor piece of work. Isabel wrote a better hand than this and she rarely misspelled a word, even in English.

Juan wrote that the Martinez family were going to Jerez. Victoria knew that already, hadn't she had a preview of Olivia's clothes and listened to the Señora babbling for hours about the marriageable young men in Jerez?

This would be an opportunity, a chance for him, Juan, to make new friends, to meet again with old friends and to be with the rest of his family; to enjoy their company and the revelry of Christmas.

Victoria turned to the second page. So far she had found nothing to justify his stupidity, his downright cruelty to that poor mule. She read on. Juan would never set foot in Navarre again, for him it was a place of disillusion, of heartbreak. She would regret her coldness, one day soon she would suffer as he had suffered, her heart would break as his had broken . . .!

Irritated by such maudlin nonsense, Victoria crushed the sheets of notepaper into a ball and flung them at the fire. Stupid, silly child! she scolded silently. Ridiculous,

selfish boy! Sending a man on a mule ten miles in this
weather to deliver pages of ill-written histrionics that
had no importance at all. She wished that he was here,
in the *sala*, she wanted to box his ears and send him out
to walk home in the rain, wind and darkness. She would
personally see to it that her son, if she had one, displayed
more common sense and thought for others. She
couldn't understand such an attitude in a young man,
and she could only conclude that Señora Martinez had
spoiled the boy from birth. Spoiled! The word stirred a
faint memory that tugged at her mind, but she couldn't
place it.

Her eye was caught by the ball of paper lying in the
otherwise immaculate hearth. Carlos brushed up the
feathery wood ash from the burned logs each time he
brought fresh fuel and the paper ball made the place
look untidy. Slowly she rose from her comfortable position on the couch. The fire was the right place for this
sick nonsense, and into the fire it should go!

The stiff paper had spread out in the heat from the
fire and as she stooped to scramble the pages together
again, words jumped out at her. 'You will weep as I
have wept'. That was plain enough, then there was an
undecipherable scrawl and the word 'revenge'. Victoria
spread the sheet out and examined it more closely.

Yes, the word was 'revenge'. What utter nonsense!
What could Juan do to her? Nothing! Surely he wasn't
stupid enough to think that he could storm the house?
Pooh! Pilar would send him flying with one sweep of a
brawny arm, or better still, Abuela would freeze him to
stone with a haughty stare down her aristocratic nose.
Juan couldn't even speak to her outside if she didn't
wish it. Nowadays, she rarely went anywhere alone.
Always either Carlos or Rafael was with her, even in
her own little car.

Rafael! Her breath caught on a gasp. Juan couldn't
hurt Rafael, could he? At that moment, the faint

memory came sweeping back. Inez! She could almost
see the tall, voluptuous figure against the door; the neg-
ligent hitch of the shoulders that brought the collar of
the mink coat against a cheek as smooth and delicately
tinted as a creamy rose petal. 'A spoiled, vicious child.'
That was what Inez had said of Juan. Fear uncoiled
itself, cold in her stomach. She flung the letter from her
as if it was a horrid insect and reached for the telephone
with a trembling hand.

With shaking fingers she dialled the number. Perhaps
the line was down—but after what seemed an eternity
she heard the ringing tone in Rafael's San Sebastian
office. It was answered immediately, but not by Rafael.
Clear over the wire came the cool, charming voice of
Señora Suarez, Rafael's efficient, middle-aged secretary,
a lady for whom he had the greatest respect, having
inherited her from his father twelve years ago and
learning nearly everything he knew about shipping and
distribution from her, or so he said.

Señora Suarez was delighted to hear from Señora
Alvarez. In elegant precise phrases she expressed her joy
and good wishes, but no, Señor Alvarez was not in the
office. He had decided to return home almost directly
after lunch. The weather might have delayed him.
Señora Suarez was leaving soon herself, her mother had
been unwell and she was anxious for her. Victoria
listened to the beautifully modulated voice, hardly hear-
ing a word except that Rafael had left early.

Good manners made her make the necessary polite
comments, but her mind was out on the road somewhere
with Rafael. If he had left early, he should have been
home long before this. Fear grew in her, poking its chilly
fingers into every nerve in her body. Juan *couldn't* harm
Rafael, could he? She thought of the big black Mercedes
parked unattended near the office where anybody could
tamper with it. Juan could have done so!

Hurriedly, she made her goodbyes and replaced the

handset before she ran as she was, in a silk blouse and a light flannel overdress, across the hall to wrench open the big door. Outside, the full force of the wind met her, flinging cold, stinging rain against her. A gust of wind slammed the door shut behind her as she ran towards the garage. Long before she reached it she was wet through, her clothes clinging wetly and her light slippers a mush of saturated velvet and fur.

Gritting her teeth, she fought to open the garage doors, whimpering as she tore her nails against the wood. They were wide heavy doors and she sobbed with fury as the wind tore them from her grasp time and time again. But at last they were opened and bolted into place.

In the darkness of the garage she could just make out the 'Noddy car'-like appearance of Emily, looking gay and workmanlike, and heaved a huge sigh of relief as she saw that Emily was pointing in the right direction and furthermore, that the keys were in the ignition. Carlos would never have given them to her had he known what she intended to do! She thanked heaven for whoever it was who had forgotten to remove those all-important keys.

There were things which she was supposed to check before she started, and in a fever of impatience she dismissed half of them as being a sheer waste of time. Oil; Carlos would have seen to that, she was sure. Petrol; Carlos always carried a full tin in the boot. Tyres; she stumbled around to the back of the car and lost a mushy slipper somewhere in the darkness of the garage. Brakes; what did she need brakes for? She was in a hurry. She would try the lights out when she was in the car, and swinging open the driver's door she scrambled in, angrily kicking off the remaining slipper.

The engine started without any fuss and Victoria found a gear, let the brake off and the clutch in with a bang. 'Emily,' she found herself praying, 'oh, Emily, don't let me down, please! If ever you've behaved yourself, behave yourself now'. Obediently the little car trundled out of the garage and down the drive, cornering at the gate so sharply that a shower of gravel was sent flying over the rose bushes in the formal beds that lined the drive.

The wipers were not nearly capable of coping with the driving rain and the storm had robbed the evening of whatever bit of daylight was left, so Victoria drove by guess and by God. Down the hill and through the village, there was nobody on the road for which she said a silent 'thank You' as she bumped and bounced over the rough cobblestones. Then the village ended and the hedgerows crowded in, making the narrow potholed road seem narrower than ever. Her face was white and fierce with concentration as she guided the little car down another hill.

The lights weren't nearly good enough and she strained to see the road in front of her. She had done this before, hadn't she? Victoria strained after the memory, and suddenly it hit her, streaking into her mind like a flash of lightning. Not this hill and not this car, a bigger hill with towering rocks on each side of its narrow width, a road that twisted back on itself in tight bends. And it wasn't this car, not her dear Emily! A much bigger car, and the big steering wheel seemed to have a mind of its own. She stamped on the brake and Emily came to a shuddering halt while she drew deep breaths and tried to clear her mind. Of all the times when her memory could have returned, this was the least convenient!

Victoria closed her eyes and shook her head as her yesterdays came crowding back into her mind. She didn't want them now! She was too busy to bother with them, she was in a hurry. Resolutely she brought her attention back to the present and took her foot from the brake, letting the little car start to roll down the hill.

Rafael was much more important than remembering, and she had to give all her attention to the road ahead.

Everything would be all right, she told herself. It had to be all right. It couldn't end now. Tears slipped down her face and she brushed them away with the back of her hand. If there had been an accident? If he was dead? Dully she thought, if Rafael was dead then she wanted to die too, but he couldn't be, she wouldn't let him! He *had* to be all right. Somebody was muttering 'Rafael, Rafael' in a funny hoarse voice and she realised it was her own voice. She shut her lips tightly and the muttering stopped and she could concentrate on the road once more.

There was this winding bit, then down the last little hill, around the corner at the bottom, up the other side and she would be on the good flat road. At the bottom of the hill she rammed her foot down on the accelerator, them moved swiftly to stamp on the brake so that Emily nearly stood upright on her droopy bonnet as a tall figure loomed up out of the driving curtain of rain that smashed against the windscreen.

Victoria flung the door open and in seconds was running barefoot along the road, stumbling on stones and stubbing her toes on the uneven surface, leaving Emily where she had stopped, but it didn't matter, nothing mattered except the tall figure walking easily towards her up the hill. Hysterically, she ran to him, her arms went round him, her hands clutching at him while tears of relief mixed with the rain that was streaming down her face. Her hair was a sodden coil that hung and dripped down her back, but she didn't care, there was warmth and reassurance in the big, warm body close against her. She would never let him go again! Never!

He was scolding as he picked her up and carried her to the shelter of the Citroën, but she didn't care about that either. She wouldn't have cared if he had cursed her in each one of the five or six languages he spoke.

Just as long as she could hear his voice close to her ear and feel his arms around her, she was quite content.

'You will explain why you are here, *querida*, without coat and shoes even. Why you are alone.' But she couldn't explain. All she could do was to reach out frantic hands and pull his head down to hers, to feel his warm, dear mouth on hers and to cling like a limpet until the fear and trembling had passed and she was warm again.

'Victoria!' There was a wry amusement in his voice and she knew that his eyes were smiling. 'Victoria, I have often wished for such a welcome as this from you, but could you not have chosen a more suitable place? No, I should know better than to ask that of you. Such a foolish question! If you are going to fling yourself into my arms, it would have to be on a lonely road, in the middle of the worst storm of the winter, and the only shelter available would be a ridiculous little car, a rattletrap on four wheels where I cannot make love to you properly. And of course we would both have to be wet through to the skin! Explanations will have to wait, *mi mujer*, while I get us back home. So sit quietly, we shall not be long.'

Emily, under far more competent hands than those of her owner, was turned round in the narrow road and then sent charging briskly up the hills and round the corners, bouncing and rattling madly over potholes and cobbles to finally enter the gates of the Casa sedately, coming to a halt by the shallow steps up to the door with an apologetic cough as the engine stopped. Her owner, bemused by happiness, accomplished the journey in complete silence for once, her hands linked about her husband's arm in a grip which, it seemed, only death would break.

She permitted herself to be carried into the house and up the stairs. Carlos, who had hurried through to the hall as they entered, was dismissed with a quick shake of Rafael's head. His offer to send up Maria was also refused. In the bedroom, Victoria struggled out of her wet clothing while Rafael ran a bath, hot, deep and foaming, for her. Casting modesty aside, she tumbled herself into it before he had even left the bathroom. She lay in the scented water with a blissful smile on her face while Rafael sought his own dressing-room to strip, shower and reclothe himself in dry garments.

Victoria's legs felt full of cotton wool when she at last levered herself out of the bath, but she had stopped trembling. Enveloped in a huge towel, she went back to the bedroom, padding across the carpeted floor and wincing now and then as her bruised feet complained at the treatment they had been given. Rafael was waiting for her, a glass of brandy ready, to give her an inner glow to match her outer one. She grimaced at the smell and took a small sip.

'Brandy,' Rafael was looking rather severe. 'Drink it up, *mi mujer*. It will prevent you having a chill.' Obediently, she drank. She didn't like the taste—but then she would cheerfully have drunk hemlock if he had told her to.

'Little fool,' he scolded gently as he rubbed her newly washed hair with a smaller towel. 'You could have killed yourself. What possessed you to do such a thing, such a mad thing? *Dios*, did you not think of the child? You could both have been killed!'

Victoria stayed quietly in his arms with an idiotic smile on her face and let his gentle rage wash over her like a healing balm. After all, it didn't matter what a loved voice said as long as it said something and she could hear it.... She didn't even bother to answer. Not yet. There would be time for that later. Now she just nuzzled her face into his chest, feeling the warm skin against her face and the prickle of springy hair against her mouth and nostrils.

'You cannot stay wrapped up in a towel for the rest

of the evening.' He brought her old green robe to her from where it was lying over the back of a chair. Victoria was feeling better now and with the return of normality, her modesty also reappeared. She took the robe from him and fled to her dressing-room, his derisive laughter followed her. 'When you feel able, I shall be expecting an explanation, and it had better be a good one, Victoria. Otherwise. . . .'

Reasonably respectable once more, Victoria re-entered the bedroom where Rafael was waiting for her. Her tongue felt glued to the roof of her mouth and the words she wanted would not come out.

'I've remembered,' she said baldly, and then, having once made a start, she found the words tripped off her tongue with no difficulty at all. They came so readily that it was not long before she found that she was no longer making sense. It was all muddled—the letter, the man and the poor wet mule, remembering; she took a deep breath and started again.

'A man came on a mule from the Martinez house—fancy sending a man and a mule in that weather!' Her voice rose in outrage. 'It was only a letter from that stupid Juan. A ridiculous letter, nothing important enough to make a man and a mule travel ten miles in that storm. . . .'

'Shall we forget about the man and the mule, *querida*? It seems to be a very sore point with you, but I am sure that neither man nor mule came to any real hurt!'

Victoria's eyes flashed green. 'I don't like cruelty to animals. I've told you that before. I think your bull-fighting is disgusting. . . .'

'We seem to be stuck on the subject of animals.' He began to sound rather vexed and Victoria blinked and fought down rising temper.

'Animals are important.' She was surly about it.

'Victoria, if I do not have a coherent story from you within one minute, I shall lose my temper.'

'Yes, I suppose you're right,' she sounded grudging, 'but it's your fault for interrupting. I'll go back to the letter. It wasn't anything really, just Juan having hysterics in pen and ink. He said that he was going to Jerez and that he would never come back, that his heart was broken. . . .'

'Where is this letter?'

'Downstairs in the *sala*, at least that's where I left it.'

'Then I had better get it and read it for myself.' Rafael smiled at her slightly. 'Otherwise we are going to be here all evening before you finally manage to tell me the whole story. Sit there quietly, *querida*, and dry your hair while I go and search the *sala* for this letter that "wasn't anything really" yet which sent you out in a storm looking for me.'

When he returned, his face was dark and forbidding and his mouth a straight line, the corners of it were tucked in with rage and his eyes glittered under his heavy lids.

'I knew he couldn't hurt me, not me personally, but I thought of you.' Victoria raised clear eyes to his. 'Forget it, Rafael. It's all over now, and he says there that he isn't coming back.'

'If he does,' his voice was an icy savage threat, 'I'll wring his insolent little neck!'

'Forget it.' Victoria managed a weak grin. 'We'll put it on the fire where it should have gone in the first place.' With gentle fingers she drew the letter from his grasp and tossed it on to the small table. 'It was silly of me to have panicked as I did. I should have known it was just Juan's adolescent hysteria, but I'd rung your office and Señora Suarez said that you'd left early, yet you were late coming home.'

'A tree across the road, *amada*. I ran into it on a bend. There was no damage done, but I could not get the car past it, so I started to walk.'

Victoria cheered up. 'It did one good thing, though.

It made me remember.' She looked at him sideways. 'I know now why I was coming back from Lourdes in such a hurry.'

'And why?'

'I love you.' The words escaped her on a soft breath.

'*Deo gratias*!' he whispered the old Latin tag against her lips. 'I have been waiting for more than a year to hear you say that!'

Over an hour later, she stirred against him, levering herself up on one elbow to study his face and to trace the line of his mouth with a proprietorial finger.

'Why did you marry me, Rafael?'

He chuckled lazily, his mouth contented. 'A business arrangement, *querida*. Surely you remember? You were so businesslike about it, staid and sedate. There were difficulties for me in the situation, you understand? I was your employer, you were living in my house. I could not make love to you as I had been wanting to do ever since you arrived from England. It would have been most improper to say the least and you might have felt— er—obligated. But Isabel had recovered, she was well and strong enough for school, so how else could I keep you with me?' He pulled her closer. 'You agreed when I suggested we marry. You had nobody, nothing to take you back to England, and Isabel loved you. You told me that she was like a small sister to you and you were happy here, so you accepted my proposal. Such a businesslike proposal, and such a formal, businesslike acceptance.' His smile was tender. 'Do you remember, *amada*? You said it was to be a proper marriage, you thought that I might want a son, and I agreed with you.'

'And what else did you do?' She quirked an eyebrow at him.

'I thanked God and took what was offered before you had a chance to change your mind. I loved you and we gave each other pleasure—you could not hide that from

me. Then I had to wait for you to discover that this was
something warmer and deeper than the mere satisfaction
of a need.'

'Oh, I did that ages ago—in fact, I've done it twice,
haven't I? Once before the accident, that was why I was
coming back from Lourdes, and then when I didn't
know you, I did it all over again. It was just that I
didn't know how you felt, you never said.' She looked
at him anxiously. 'By the way, have I been a satisfactory
wife or have I been a disappointment to you?'

'Eminently satisfactory.' Beneath her cheek she could
feel the laughter rumbling in his chest. 'I have been
shocked, maddened and stunned, sometimes made mad
with frustration, but I have never been disappointed,
never!'

'Mmm,' Victoria slid her arms round his neck, 'I've
always found you most satisfactory too.' She said it
simply, like a child, but her eyes were not a child's eyes.

Carlos chose this moment to sound the gong for
dinner, so that she sprang up hastily, reaching for the
robe which had been discarded at some time, she
couldn't remember just when. She rushed to the wardrobe, explaining as she feverishly sought for a dress,

'If we don't go down, Pilar will come up here searching for me. She's convinced that I don't eat enough and
the poor baby will be as thin and small as a tadpole.'
She scrambled herself into the green caftan, brushed and
tied back her hair with a chiffon scarf and pushed her
feet into soft sandals.

'There, will I do?' She raised wide eyes to Rafael's
and returned his kiss enthusiastically. 'At least,' she
pointed out as they went down the stairs, 'love's not
like Pilar's dinner. It won't be spoiled by being kept
back for an hour or so, will it?'

On a cold, wet day in January, Victoria sat by the fire
in the *sala*, her face pale and mutinous. Isabel was to go

to Amsterdam the next week. Rafael was taking her and he would have to stay with her, no matter how long the treatment took, and he had flatly refused to allow her to go with them.

'Lots of women go travelling when they're pregnant,' she had protested. 'I don't see why I should have to be left behind. You could be there a month, perhaps longer, and the baby's not due to be born until late March or early April. Anybody would think that I would be likely to have it on a bus!'

Her protests and spurts of temper had no effect whatsoever. Rafael ignored them all. She sighed with exasperation; it was her own fault. If she had wanted a nice, easygoing husband, she should never have married Rafael—and, she gloomed, it wasn't any use trying to pretend that she hadn't known what he was like before she had married him, because she had. Twice! The second time had been in the hospital, when he had appeared as a stranger to her. She had known then that he would walk all over her.

The click of the door latch made her turn her head.

'Happy New Year, little cousin,' said Inez as if she had never been away, never gone to live in Madrid.

'Inez!' Victoria could not hide her surprise. 'I thought you were whooping it up in Madrid.'

'I was, and I will be again.' The red mouth curved into a charming smile. 'I've just had word that an American firm wants to buy my house. The firm runs a chain of hotels throughout Europe and they want one in Madrid. I believe I have to thank Abuela and Rafael for the deal.' Again, Inez smiled.

'But why are you here?' Victoria was being wary of this new Inez.

'Mainly to wish you well, little cousin.' Inez tossed furs on to a nearby chair and came to hold out an elegant, slender hand to warm her fingers. 'But just now, somebody has to go with Isabel and stay with her, and you obviously can't.' She allowed her eyes to wander pointedly over Victoria's swollen figure. 'Abuela told me about it in her last letter. I shall be a poor substitute for you and Rafael, but I'll do my best, and at the very least, I'll be a familiar face. I've often thought of a little holiday in Holland, it's the windmills, I think. You never know, I might find Dutchmen irresistible.' Again came the smile, and this time with real amusement. 'No, don't rush about telling everybody that I'm here, they already know.'

'Fancy Inez deserting Madrid to take Isabel!' Victoria turned to her husband as she made ready for bed.

Rafael's eyebrows lifted in surprise. 'You can't go and Abuela can't either. I could, but it would be very difficult. What else did you expect?' He sounded reasonable.

'But she's so kind, so different.' Victoria remembered the little barbs, but now it was with amusement.

'Inez is happy.' He stroked her hair tenderly. 'People change when they're happy and Inez is going to sell her house, which will give her some extra capital. Also I think that perhaps she has a very good reason for wanting to go to Amsterdam, a reason that has little to do with Isabel.'

'I shall be very glad to see my feet again,' Victoria murmured inconsequentially. 'I haven't seen them for ages.' She felt clumsy as she hoisted herself into the bed.

Rafael eyed her thoughtfully as she made herself comfortable. 'I think, if you are well enough, that we will have a little holiday. We will go to Granada for a week or so while Inez and Isabel are away. It is still winter, but it will be warmer there. We can telephone Amsterdam as well from Granada as we can from here and speak to Isabel every day.'

'That's marvellous!' She eyed him admiringly. 'I must say that I like the way you cope with your divided loyalties.'

'Isabel, I can trust,' he looked at her with a sly

amusement. 'She is sane, sensible, well balanced. . . .'

He did not finish the sentence; his wife threw a pillow at him.

Granada was beautiful and it was warmer there, although the snow still lay thick on the Sierras Nevadas. Already it seemed that spring was coming. Victoria loved every minute of their stay there, she loved the quiet secretiveness of the houses, especially the old ones, which presented bland blind faces to the world, hiding their fountains and courtyards behind screens of wrought iron. And there was so much water! It seemed to her that Granada tinkled with the noise of fountains. But after two weeks she became uneasy.

'Do you not like Granada?' Rafael looked puzzled as she came from the telephone after a long call to Abuela.

'Of course I like it, but I want to go home. I miss the Casa and Abuela, even Sancha's eternal worrying and moaning. I want to be there for when Isabel arrives.'

'That will not be for another month at least,' he pointed out reasonably. 'The weather will be bad there, it always is at this time of the year. Storms blow in from the bay and we get more than our fair share of rain.'

'I like rain.' She was perverse. 'I like storms and I like the Casa. We can always come back here later. I've seen enough fountains and gardens for the time being. Let's go home, please.'

Rafael snorted and made rude remarks about the stupidity of women in general and one in particular, but privately Victoria thought he seemed rather pleased, and home they went, to arrive in a downpour of rain and a brisk chill wind that blew her skirt about her legs and her hair all over her face.

Now it was April and through the bedroom windows she could see white clouds scudding across a pale blue sky. She was very tired but content.

Rafael had left for San Sebastian that morning un-aware of how close they were to the big event. Victoria didn't want him to know, he'd start ordering people about and being kind, solicitous, tender and bossy. This, she had decided, she preferred to do on her own.

As his car passed through the gates of the Casa, she sent Carlos to phone for Dr Garcia and then bit her lip as she admitted to herself that she had got the timing wrong. Long before the plump little doctor could be expected to arrive, Felipe Rafael Alvarez came, aided only by Pilar, who had taken one look at Victoria's face and, yelling, had sent Maria scurrying for the usual hot water and towels.

Victoria looked at the little head covered in black down and smiled triumphantly. Carlos would have been on the phone to San Sebastian as soon as Pilar gave the first yell, but with the best will in the world Rafael could not be back here in less than two hours. The doctor had been and gone, pronouncing himself to be quite satisfied with their efforts, and now she would have a nice cup of tea and doze until Rafael arrived.

'Tea!' she demanded of a joyous Pilar, and fell asleep before it could be made.

A movement of the bed awoke her. Rafael was there and the room was full of the scent of flowers.

'You sent me away this morning,' he accused haughtily. 'Why did you not tell me?'

'I thought I'd surprise you,' Victoria grinned at him. 'My book on the subject says that the presence of the father is not necessary at times like this, and the book was quite right. We didn't even need the doctor. Pilar and I managed splendidly. Are you pleased?' There was a faintly anxious note in her voice, but what she saw in his eyes was infinitely reassuring.

His arm came about her as she struggled to sit up in the bed and she smiled at him as if this was quite an ordinary day.

'It was quite all right, and not half as frightening as I thought it might be.' Her gaze lingered, not on her son but on his father. 'We'll have to do it again some time,' she told him sedately.

Pilar came in with a fresh pot of tea and cooed stentoriously at the baby while Rafael poured.

Over the rim of her cup, Victoria laughed at him, then suddenly became serious. 'I love you,' she whispered. 'Is it still the same with you?'

Against her ear, his voice came soft. *'Por toda mi vida.'*

'Nice,' thought Victoria, but she wasn't going to kid herself. Rafael might be tender and considerate now, but it wouldn't last. In a very short time he would revert to his usual domineering, arrogant ways.

'Isabel will be very happy and pleased,' she told him. 'She particularly wanted a brother.'

'And you, *querida*, are you happy and pleased?'

Victoria put her head down on the chest of her arrogant, male chauvinist pig of a husband and sighed with content.

'Very!'

MAD BULLS AND SPANISH MEN...

It is dawn of the seventh of July. The sun rises over the foothills of the Pyrenees and sets afire the red tile roofs of Pamplona, ancient capital of the northern Spanish province of Navarre. At 7:00 A.M. the air is still cool, but it will warm quickly as the sun mounts in the sky. Already the narrow winding streets in the town's medieval quarter are thronged with people. For this is the opening day of the Feast of St. Firminus, a two-week festival that celebrates the appointment of Pamplona's first native-born bishop a thousand years ago.

The crowd has an air of excited expectancy. Suddenly from around the corner of high stucco houses appear some fifty young men, wearing the yellow sashes of Navarre. Yelling and whooping almost as if in a drunken frenzy, they run as fast as their legs can carry them. A dozen bulls, black and brawny creatures with powerful heads and deadly horns, pound behind them. This is the first day of the Pamplones' favorite festival activity—the *encierro*, or "running of the bulls."

The men turn and dance in front of the charging angry animals, allowing them to come within a hairbreadth before dashing off again, the beasts close on their heels. Side streets have been blocked by fences, but in some wide intersections spectators line the sidewalks, kept from danger by the running men, who eagerly distract the bulls from the crowd.

Finally the men and the bulls reach their destination, a corral outside Pamplona's bullfighting arena. The bulls will be watered and rested to await their fate later in the day in the bullring.

And the young men will go off to sleep to prepare themselves for a long evening of festivities—and the next day's running of the bulls!

Your FREE gift includes

- *Anne Hampson* — Beyond the Sweet Waters
- *Anne Mather* — The Arrogant Duke
- *Violet Winspear* — Cap Flamingo
- *Nerina Hilliard* — Teachers Must Learn